SIMON RAVEN

The Judas Boy

PANTHER
Granada Publishing

Panther Books
Granada Publishing Ltd
8 Grafton Street, London W1X 3LA

Published by Panther Books 1969
Reprinted 1971, 1979, 1985

First published in Great Britain by
Anthony Blond Ltd 1968

Copyright © Simon Raven 1968

ISBN 0-586-02883-8

Printed and bound in Great Britain by
Collins, Glasgow

Set in Linotype Times

Simon Raven was born in London in 1927. He was educated at Charterhouse and King's College, Cambridge where he read Classics. After university, he joined the army as a regular officer in the King's Shropshire Light Infantry and saw service in Germany and Kenya where he commanded a Rifle Company. In 1957 he resigned his commission and took up book reviewing. His first novel, *The Feathers of Death*, was published in 1959. Since then he has written many reviews, general essays, plays for radio and television as well as the scripts for a number of successful television series including *Edward and Mrs Simpson* and *Love in a Cold Climate* plus a host of novels. The highly acclaimed ALMS FOR OBLIVION sequence is published for the first time in this Panther edition in chronological order. The sequence takes its title from a passage in Shakespeare's *Troilus and Cressida*, has been referred to as 'a latter-day Waugh report on another generation of Bright Young Things', and has been compared favourably with the *romans fleuves* of Anthony Powell and C. P. Snow. With the publication in 1984 of *Morning Star* he began a new novel series under the title THE FIRST BORN OF EGYPT. It is a sequel to ALMS FOR OBLIVION. Simon Raven lives and works in Deal, Kent.

By the same author

Novels

The Feathers of Death
Brother Cain
Doctors Wear Scarlet
Close of Play
The Fortunes of Fingel

The ALMS FOR OBLIVION sequence,
in chronological order:

Fielding Gray
Sound the Retreat
The Sabre Squadron
The Rich Pay Late
Friends in Low Places
The Judas Boy
Places Where They Sing
Come Like Shadows
Bring Forth the Body
The Survivors

Essays

The English Gentleman
Boys Will Be Boys

Plays

Royal Foundation and Other Plays

Contents

PRINCIPAL CHARACTERS IN
ALMS FOR OBLIVION

The *Alms for Oblivion* sequence consists of ten novels. They are, in chronological order: *Fielding Gray* (FG), set in 1945; *Sound the Retreat* (SR), 1945–6; *The Sabre Squadron* (SS), 1952; *The Rich Pay Late* (RPL), 1955–6; *Friends in Low Places* (FLP), 1959; *The Judas Boy* (JB), 1962; *Places Where They Sing* (PWTS), 1967; *Come Like Shadows* (CLS), 1970; *Bring Forth the Body* (BFB), 1972; and *The Survivors* (TS), 1973.

What follows is an alphabetical list of the more important characters, showing in which of the novels they have each appeared and briefly suggesting their roles.

Albani, Euphemia: daughter of Fernando Albani *q.v.* (TS).

Albani, Fernando: Venetial merchant of late 18th and early 19th centuries. Author of manuscripts researched by Fielding Gray *q.v.* in 1973 (TS).

Albani, Maria: wife to Fernando (TS).

Albani, Piero: son of Fernando (TS). Not to be confused with the Piero *q.v.* of no known surname who lives with Lykiadopoulos in Venice in 1973 (TS).

Balliston, Hugh: an undergraduate of Lancaster College, Cambridge in 1967 (PWTS); retreats to a convent of Franciscan Friars near Venice, and is recognized in Venice by Daniel Mond in 1973 (TS).

Beatty, Miss: a secretary in the firm of Salinger & Holbrook (RPL). †1956 (RPL).

Beck, Tony: a young Fellow of Lancaster College, well known as a literary critic (PWTS).

Beyfus, The Lord (life Peer): a social scientist, Fellow of Lancaster College (PWTS).

Blakeney, Balbo: a biochemist, Fellow of Lancaster College (PWTS); still a Fellow of Lancaster and present at Daniel Mond's funeral in 1973 (TS).

Blessington, Ivan: a school friend of Fielding Gray in 1945 (FG) later a regular officer in the 49th Earl Hamilton's Light Dragoons (Hamilton's Horse); ADC to his Divisional Commander in Germany in 1952 (SS); by 1955 an attaché at the British Embassy in Washington (RPL); by 1972 retired from the army and working at high level for a prominent merchant bank (BFB); pensioned off from the bank for indiscretion in 1973 (TS).

von Bremke, Herr Doktor Aeneas: a prominent mathematician

at the University of Göttingen (SS).

Brockworthy, Lieutenant-Colonel: Commanding Officer of the 1st Battalion, the Wessex Fusiliers, at Berhampore in 1946 (SR).

Bunce, Basil: Squadron Sergeant-Major of the 10th Sabre Squadron of Earl Hamilton's Light Dragoons at Göttingen in 1952 (SS), and on Santa Kytherea in 1955 (FG); present at Daniel Mond's funeral in 1973 (TS).

Bungay, Piers: Subaltern officer of the 10th Sabre Squadron at Göttingen in 1952 (SS).

Buttock, Mrs Tessie: owner of Buttock's Hotel in the Cromwell Road (RPL, FLP, JB, CLS), a convenient establishment much favoured by Tom Llewyllyn and Fielding Gray *q.v.*

Canteloupe, The Marchioness (Molly): wife of The Marquis Canteloupe (FLP, SR).

CANTELOUPE, The Most Honourable the Marquis: father of The Earl of Muscateer (SR); distant cousin of Captain Detterling *q.v.* and political associate of Somerset Lloyd-James *q.v.*; successful operator of his 'Stately Home' and in 1959 Parliamentary Secretary for the Development of British Recreational Resources (FLP); Minister of Public Relations and Popular Media in 1962 (JB); Shadow Minister of Commerce in 1967 (PWTS); Minister of Commerce in the Conservative Government of 1970 (CLS); still Minister in 1972, though under heavy pressure (BFB). †1973 (TS).

Carnavon, Angus: leading male star in Pandarus/Clytemnestra Film Production of *The Odyssey* on Corfu in 1970 (CLS).

Carnwath, Doctor: a Cambridge don and historian; an old friend of Provost Constable, and a member of the Lauderdale Committee; †early 1950s (BFB).

Chead, 'Corpy': Corporal-Major (*i.e.* Colour Sergeant) of the 10th Sabre Squadron at Göttingen (SS); present at Daniel Mond's funeral in 1973 (TS).

Clewes, The Reverend Oliver: Chaplain to Lancaster College (PWTS).

CONSTABLE, Robert Reculver (Major): demobilized with special priority in the summer of 1945 to take up appointment as Tutor of Lancaster College, Cambridge (FG); by 1955 Vice-Chancellor of the University of Salop, and *ex officio* member of the Board of *Strix* (RPL); elected Provost of Lancaster in 1959 (FLP); still Provost in 1962 (JB) and 1967 (PWTS) and 1972 (BFB); ennobled as Lord Constable of Reculver Castle in 1973 (TS).

Corrington, Mona: an anthropologist, Fellow of Girton College, Cambridge, Chum of Lord Beyfus *q.v.* (PWTS).

Cruxtable, Sergeant-Major: Company Sergeant-Major of Peter Morrison's Company at the O.T.S., Bangalore, in 1945-6 (SR); 'P.T. expert' at Canteloupe's physical fitness camp in the west country (FLP).

DETTERLING, Captain: distant cousin of Lord Canteloupe; regular officer of The 49th Earl Hamilton's Light Dragoons (Hamilton's Horse) from 1937; in charge of recruiting for the Cavalry in 1945 (FG); instructor at the O.T.S., Bangalore, from late 1945 to summer 1946 (SR); by 1952 has retired from Hamilton's Horse and become a Member of Parliament (SS); still M.P. in 1955 and a political supporter of Peter Morrison *q.v.* (RPL); still M.P. in 1959, when he joins Gregory Stern *q.v.* as a partner in Stern's publishing house (FLP); still M.P. and publisher in 1962 (JB) and 1970 (CLS), and 1972, at which time he gives important assistance to those enquiring into the death of Somerset Lloyd-James (BFB); inherits his distant cousin Canteloupe's marquisate by special remainder in 1973 (TS), and insists that the spelling of the title now be changed to 'marquess'.

Dexterside, Ashley: friend and employee of Donald Salinger (RPL).

Dharaparam, H.H. The Maharajah of: an Indian Prince; Patron of the Cricket Club of the O.T.S., Bangalore (SR).

Dilkes, Henry: Secretary to the Institute of Political and Economic Studies and a member of the Board of *Strix* (RPL, FLP).

Dixon, Alastair: Member of Parliament for safe Conservative seat in the west country; about to retire in 1959 (FLP), thus creating a vacancy coveted both by Peter Morrison and Somerset Lloyd-James *q.v.*

Dolly: maid of all work to Somerset Lloyd-James in his chambers in Albany (BFB).

Drew, Vanessa: *v.* Salinger, Donald.

Engineer, Margaret Rose: a Eurasian harlot who entertains Peter Morrison *q.v.* in Bangalore (SR).

fitzAvon, Humbert: otherwise called Lord Rollesden-in-Silvis, the man with whom the manuscripts of Fernando Albani *q.v.* are principally concerned (TS).

de FREVILLE, Max: gambler and connoisseur of human affairs; runs big chemin-de-fer games in the London of the fifties (RPL), maintaining a private spy-ring for protection from possible welshers and also for the sheer amusement of it (FLP); later goes abroad to Venice, Hydra, Cyprus and

Corfu, where he engages in various enterprises (FLP, JB, CLS), often in partnership with Lykiadopoulos *q.v.* and usually attended by Angela Tuck *q.v.* His Corfiot interests include a share in the 1970 Pandarus/Clytemnestra production of *The Odyssey* (CLS); still active in Corfu in 1972 (BFB); still in partnership with Lykiadopoulos, whom he accompanies to Venice in the autumn of 1973 (TS).

Frith, Hetta: girl friend of Hugh Balliston *q.v.* (PWTS). † 1967 (PWTS).

Galahead, Foxe J. (Foxy): Producer for Pandarus and Clytemnestra Films of *The Odyssey* on Corfu in 1970 (CLS).

Gamp, Jonathan: a not so young man about town (RPL, FLP, BFB).

Gilzai Khan, Captain: an Indian officer (Moslem) holding the King's Commission; an instructor at the O.T.S., Bangalore, 1945–6; resigns to become a political agitator (SR). †1946 (SR).

Glastonbury, Major Giles: an old friend of Detterling *q.v.* and regular officer of Hamilton's Horse; temporary Lieutenant-Colonel on Lord Wavell's staff in India 1945–6 (SR); officer commanding the 10th Sabre Squadron of Hamilton's Horse at Göttingen in 1952 (SS).

Grange, Lady Susan: marries Lord Philby (RPL).

Gray, John Aloysius (Jack): Fielding Gray's father (FG). †1945.

Gray, Mrs: Fielding Gray's mother (FG). † *c.* 1948.

GRAY, Major Fielding: senior schoolboy in 1945 (FG) with Peter Morrison and Somerset Lloyd-James *q.v.*; scholar elect of Lancaster College, but tangles with the authorities, is deprived of his scholarship before he can take it up (FG), and becomes a regular officer of Earl Hamilton's Light Dragoons; 2 i/c and then O.C. the 10th Sabre Squadron in Göttingen in 1952 (SS) and still commanding the Squadron on Santa Kytherea in 1955 (KG); badly mutilated in Cyprus in 1958 and leaves the Army to become critic and novelist with the help of Somerset Lloyd-James (FLP); achieves minor distinction, and in 1962 is sent out to Greece and Cyprus by Tom Llewyllyn *q.v.* to investigate Cypriot affairs, past and present, for BBC Television (JB); in Greece meets Harriet Ongley *q.v.*; by 1967 has won the Joseph Conrad Prize for Fiction (PWTS); goes to Corfu in 1970 to rewrite script for Pandarus/Clytemnestra's *The Odyssey* (CLS); in 1972 is engaged on a study of Joseph Conrad, which is to be published, as part of a new series, by Gregory Stern (BFB); derives considerable financial benefit from the Conrad book, and settles temporarily in Venice in the autumn of 1973 (TS).

His researches into a by-water of Venetian history cause trouble among his friends and provide himself with the material for a new novel.

Grimes, Sasha: a talented young actress playing in Pandarus/Clytemnestra's *The Odyssey* on Corfu (CLS).

The Headmaster of Fielding Gray's School (FG): a man of conscience.

Helmutt, Jacquiz: historian; research student at Lancaster College in 1952 (SS); later Fellow of Lancaster (PWTS); still a Fellow of Lancaster and present at Daniel Mond's funeral in 1973 (TS).

Holbrook, Jude: partner of Donald Salinger *q.v.* 1949–56 (RPL); 'freelance' in 1959 (FLP); reported by Burke Lawrence *q.v.* (CLS) as having gone to live in Hong Kong in the sixties; discovered to have retired, with his mother, to a villa in the Veneto 1973 (TS), having apparently enriched himself in Hong Kong.

Holbrook, Penelope: a model; wife of Jude Holbrook (RPL); by 1959, divorced from Jude and associated with Burke Lawrence (FLP); reported by Burke Lawrence (CLS) as still living in London and receiving alimony from Jude in Hong Kong.

Holeworthy, R.S.M.: Regimental Sergeant-Major of the Wessex Fusiliers at Göttingen in 1952 (SS).

Jacobson, Jules: old hand in the film world; Director of Pandarus/Clytemnestra's *The Odyssey* on Corfu in 1970 (CLS).

James, Cornet Julian: Cambridge friend of Daniel Mond *q.v.*; in 1952 a National Service officer of the 10th Sabre Squadron at Göttingen (SS).

Joe: groundsman at Detterling's old school (BFB).

Lamprey, Jack: a subaltern officer of the 10th Sabre Squadron (SS).

La Soeur, Doctor: a confidential practitioner, physician to Fielding Gray (FG, RPL, CLS).

Lawrence, Burke: 'film director' and advertising man (RPL); from *c.* 1956 to 1959 teams up with Penelope Holbrook *q.v.* in murky 'agency' (FLP); *c.* 1960 leaves England for Canada, and later becomes P.R.O. to Clytemnestra Films (CLS).

Lewson, Felicity: born Contessina Felicula Maria Monteverdi; educated largely in England; wife of Mark Lewson (though several years his senior) and his assistant in his profession (RPL). †1959 (FLP).

Lewson, Mark: a con man (RPL, FLP). †1959 (FLP).

Lichfield, Margaret: star actress playing Penelope in the Pandarus/Clytemnestra production of *The Odyssey* on Corfu in 1970 (CLS).

LLEWYLLYN, Tom: a 'scholarship boy' of low Welsh origin but superior education; author, journalist and contributor to *Strix* (RPL); same but far more successful by 1959, when he marries Patricia Turbot *q.v.* (FLP); given important contract by BBC Television in 1962 to produce *Today is History*, and later that year appointed Namier Fellow of Lancaster College (JB); renewed as Namier Fellow in 1965 and still at Lancaster in 1967 (PWTS); later made a permanent Fellow of the College (CLS); employed by Pandarus and Clytemnestra Films as 'Literary and Historical Adviser' to their production of *The Odyssey* on Corfu in 1970 (CLS); still a don at Lancaster in 1972, when he is reported to be winning esteem for the first volume of his *magnum opus* (published by the Cambridge University Press) on the subject of Power (BFB); comes to Venice in the autumn of 1973 (TS), nominally to do research but in fact to care for Daniel Mond.

Llewyllyn, Tullia: always called and known as 'Baby'; Tom and Patricia's daughter, born in 1960 (JB, PWTS, CLS, BFB); on the removal from the scene of her mother, is sent away to school in the autumn of 1973 (TS). Becomes a close friend of Captain Detterling, now Marquess Canteloupe.

Lloyd-James, Mrs Peregrina: widowed mother of Somerset Lloyd-James (BFB).

LLOYD-JAMES, Somerset: a senior schoolboy and friend of Fielding Gray in 1945 (FG); by 1955, Editor of *Strix*, an independent economic journal (RPL); still editor of *Strix* in 1959 (FPL) and now seeking a seat in Parliament; still editor of *Strix* in 1962 (JB), but now also a Member of Parliament and unofficial adviser to Lord Canteloupe *q.v.*; still M.P. and close associate of Canteloupe in 1967 (PWTS), and by 1970 Canteloupe's official understrapper in the House of Commons (CLS), still so employed in 1972 (BFB), with the title of Parliamentary Under-Secretary of State at the Ministry of Commerce; †1972 (BFB).

Lykiadopoulos, Stratis: a Greek gentleman, or not far off it; professional gambler and a man of affairs (FLP) who has a brief liaison with Mark Lewson; friend and partner of Max de Freville *q.v.* (FLP), with whom he has business interests in Cyprus (JB) and later in Corfu (CLS); comes to Venice in the autumn of 1973 (TS) to run a Baccarat Bank and thus prop up his fortunes in Corfu, which are now rather shaky. Is accompanied by Max de Freville *q.v.* and a Sicilian boy called Piero *q.v.*

Maisie: a whore (RPL, FLP, JB) frequented with enthusiasm by Fielding Gray, Lord Canteloupe and Somerset Lloyd-James; apparently still going strong as late as 1967 (ref. PWTS) and even 1970 (ref. CLS), and 1972 (BFB).

Mayerston: a revolutionary (PWTS).

Mond, Daniel: a mathematician; research student of Lancaster College (SS) sent to Göttingen University in 1952 to follow up his line of research, which unexpectedly turns out to have a military potential; later Fellow of Lancaster and teacher of pure mathematics (PWTS). †in Venice in 1973 (TS).

Morrison, Helen: Peter Morrison's wife (RPL, FLP, BFB).

MORRISON, Peter: senior schoolboy with Fielding Gray and Somerset Lloyd-James *q.v.* in 1945 (FG); an officer cadet at the O.T.S., Bangalore, from late 1945 to summer 1946 (SR) and then commissioned as a Second Lieutenant in the Wessex Fusiliers, whom he joins at Berhampore; by 1952 has inherited substantial estates in East Anglia and by 1955 is a Member of Parliament (RPL) where he leads 'the Young England Group'; but in 1956 applies for Chiltern Hundreds (RPL); tries and fails to return to Parliament in 1959 (FLP); reported by Lord Canteloupe (CLS) as having finally got a seat again after a by-election in 1968 and as having retained it at the General Election in 1970; in 1972 appointed Parliamentary Under-Secretary of State at the Ministry of Commerce on the demise of Somerset Lloyd-James (BFB); appointed Minister of Commerce on death of Lord Canteloupe *q.v.* in 1973 (TS); soon after is in Venice to take a hand in industrial intrigues in Mestre.

Morrison, 'Squire': Peter's father (FG), owner of a fancied racehorse (Tiberius). † *c.* 1950.

Mortleman, Alister: an officer cadet at the O.T.S., Bangalore, 1945–6, later commissioned into the Wessex Fusiliers (SR).

Motley, Mick: Lieutenant of the R.A.M.C., attached to the Wessex Fusiliers at Göttingen in 1952 (SS).

Murphy, 'Wanker': an officer cadet at the O.T.S., Bangalore, 1945–6; later commissioned as Captain in the Education Corps, then promoted to be Major and Galloper to the Viceroy of India (SR). †1946 (SR).

Muscateer, Earl of: son of Lord and Lady Canteloupe *q.v.*; an officer cadet at the O.T.S., Bangalore, 1945–6 (SR). †1946 (SR).

Nicos: a Greek boy who picks up Fielding Gray (JB).

Ogden, The Reverend Andrew: Dean of the Chapel of Lancaster College (PWTS).

Ongley, Mrs Harriet: rich American widow; Fielding Gray's mistress and benefactress from 1962 onwards (JB, PWTS, CLS), but has left him by 1972 (BFB).

Pappenheim, Herr: German ex-officer of World War II; in 1952 about to rejoin new West German Army as a senior staff officer (SS).

Percival, Leonard: cloak-and-dagger man; in 1952 nominally a Lieutenant of the Wessex Fusiliers at Göttingen (SS), but by 1962 working strictly in plain clothes (JB); friend of Max de Freville, with whom he occasionally exchanges information to their mutual amusement (JB); transferred to a domestic department ('Jermyn Street') of the secret service and rated 'Home enquiries only', because of stomach ulcers in 1972, when he investigates, in association with Detterling, the death of Somerset Lloyd-James (BFB); joins Detterling (now Lord Canteloupe) in Venice in 1973 in order to investigate a 'threat' to Detterling (TS). Becomes Detterling's personal secretary and retires from 'Jermyn Street'.

Percival, Rupert: a small-town lawyer in the west country (FLP), prominent among local Conservatives and a friend of Alistair Dixon q.v.; Leonard Percival's uncle (JB).

Philby, The Lord: proprietor of *Strix* (RPL, FLP) which he has inherited along with his title from his father, 'old' Philby.

Piero: A Sicilian boy who accompanies Lykiadopoulos q.v. to Venice in 1973 (TS). Becomes friend of Daniel Mond. Not to be confused with Piero Albani q.v.

Pough (pronounced Pew), The Honourable Grantchester Fitz-Margrave: Senior Fellow of Lancaster College, Professor Emeritus of Oriental Geography, at one time celebrated as a mountaineer; a dietary fadist (PWTS).

Pulcher, Detective Sergeant: assistant to Detective Superintendent Stupples, q.v. (BFB).

Restarick, Earle: American cloak-and-dagger man; in 1952 apparently a student at Göttingen University (SS) but in fact taking an unwholesome interest in the mathematical researches of Daniel Mond q.v.; later active in Cyprus (JB) and in Greece (CLS); at Mestre in autumn of 1973 in order to assist with American schemes for the industrialization of the area (TS); present at Daniel Mond's funeral.

Roland, Christopher: a special school friend of Fielding Gray (FG). †1945 (FG).

Salinger, Donald: senior partner of Salinger & Holbrook, a printing firm (RPL); in 1956 marries Vanessa Drew (RPL);

is deserted by Jude Holbrook *q.v.* in the summer of 1956 (RPL) but in 1959 is still printing (FLP), and still married to Vanessa; in 1972 is reported as having broken down mentally and retired to a private Nursing Home in consequence of Vanessa's death by drowning (BFB).

Schottgatt, Doctor Emile: of Montana University, Head of the 'Creative Authentication Committee' of the Oglander-Finckelstein Trust, which visits Corfu in 1970 (CLS) to assess the merits of the Pandarus/Clytemnestra production of *The Odyssey*.

Schroeder, Alfie: a reporter employed by the Billingsgate Press (RPL, FLP, SS); by 1967 promoted to columnist (PWTS); 'famous' as columnist by 1973, when he attends Daniel Mond's funeral (TS).

Sheath, Aloysius: a scholar on the staff of the American School of Greek Studies in Athens, but also assistant to Earle Restarick *q.v.* (JB, CLS).

Stern, Gregory: publisher (RPL), later in partnership with Captain Detterling *q.v.* (FLP); publishes Tom Llewyllyn and Fielding Gray *q.v.* (RPL, FLP, JB, PWTS, CLS); married to Isobel Turbot (FLP); still publishing in 1973 (TS), by which time Isobel has persuaded him into vulgar and profitable projects.

Strange, Barry: an officer cadet at the O.T.S., Bangalore, 1945–6, later commissioned into the Wessex Fusiliers, with whom he has strong family connections (SR).

Stupples, Detective Superintendent: policeman initially responsible for enquiries into the death of Somerset Lloyd-James in 1972 (BFB).

Tuck: a tea-planter in India; marries Angela, the daughter of a disgraced officer, and brings her back to England in 1945 (FG); later disappears, but turns up as an official of the Control Commission in Germany in 1952 (SS). †1956 (RPL).

TUCK, Mrs Angela: daughter of a Colonel in the Indian Army Pay Corps, with whom she lives in Southern India (JB, FLP) until early 1945, when her father is dismissed the Service for malversation; being then *in extremis* marries Tuck the tea-planter, and returns with him to England in the summer of 1945 (FG); briefly mistress to the adolescent Somerset Lloyd-James *q.v.*, and to 'Jack' Gray (Fielding's father); despite this a trusted friend of Fielding's mother (FG); by 1955 is long separated from Tuck and now mistress to Jude Holbrook (RPL); in 1956 inherits small fortune from the intestate Tuck, from whom she has never been actually divorced *pace* her bibulous and misleading soliloquies on the subject in the text (RPL); in 1959 living in Menton and occasional companion of Max de Freville *q.v.* (FLP); later Max's constant companion (JB, CLS). †1970 (CLS).

Turbot, The Right Honourable Sir Edwin, P.C., Kt: politician; in 1946 ex-Minister of wartime coalition accompanying all-party delegation of M.P.s to India (SR); by 1959 long since a Minister once more, and 'Grand Vizier' of the Conservative Party (FLP); father of Patricia, who marries Tom Llewyllyn (FLP), and of Isobel, who marries Gregory Stern (FLP); by 1962 reported as badly deteriorating and as having passed some of his fortune over to his daughters (JB). †by 1967 (PWTS), having left more money to his daughters.

Turbot, Isobel: *v.* Turbot, Sir Edwin, and Stern, Gregory.

Turbot, Patricia: *v.* Turbot, Sir Edwin, and Llewyllyn, Tom. Also *v.* Llewyllyn, Tullia. Has brief walk-out with Hugh Balliston *q.v.* (PWTS) and is disobliging to Tom about money (JB, PWTS, CLS). In 1972 is reported by Jonathan Gamp to be indulging in curious if not criminal sexual preferences (BFB); as a result of these activities is finally overtaken by disaster and put away in an asylum in 1973 (TS), much to the benefit of her husband and daughter.

Weekes, James: bastard son of Somerset Lloyd-James, born in 1946 (BFB).

Weekes, Mrs Meriel: *quondam* and random associate of Somerset Lloyd-James, and mother of his bastard son (BFB).

Weir, Carton: Member of Parliament and political associate of Peter Morrison (RPL); later official aide to Lord Canteloupe (FLP, JB). P.P.S. to Canteloupe at Ministry of Commerce in 1972 (BFB); becomes P.P.S. to Peter Morrison *q.v.* when the latter takes over as Minister of Commerce on the death of Lord Canteloupe.

Winstanley, Ivor: a distinguished Latinist, Fellow of Lancaster College (PWTS).

'Young bastard': assistant groundsman at Detterling's old school (BFB).

Zaccharias: an officer cadet at the O.T.S., Bangalore, 1945–6; commissioned into a dowdy regiment of the line (SR).

AUTHOR'S NOTE

For the purposes of this novel, certain characters are supposedly employed by the British Broadcasting Corporation. Neither the characters themselves nor the 'appointments' which they hold have any connection at all with actual persons or appointments within the Corporation as it is presently constituted or has been constituted at any time during its past. In real life, for example, I understand that the BBC comprehends a Head of Features Group, a Head of Science and Features, and a Head of Arts Features; but none of these has anything whatever to do with my 'Director of Features', whose persona, title and function are totally fictitious. Similarly, 'Miss Enid Jackson' of 'Administration' is a complete invention.

S.R.

Part 1: The Island of Love

Trapped, he thought: there is no way out of this coach and there is certain death waiting inside it. Think. You have thirty seconds (with luck) to think.

But how could he offer resistance to an enemy that was invisible, impalpable? *A piece on a chess board can offer no resistance because it is caught in a situation which has been devised by a mental power totally remote from itself. Except by that power the situation is unalterable; and so was the situation in which he himself was trapped now. It was of mathematical exactness, it could be represented by a classical syllogism: To stay is to die; but it is impossible not to stay; therefore it is impossible not to die.*

Don't trifle, man: think. Unlike a piece on a chess board, you have a certain power of motion. You can at least move about within the square on which you are trapped. That square is this train, or rather, this coach. Move about it, dodge the enemy. But move where? Down the corridor. The enemy is waiting there too. Then move back again. Whatever you do, don't stay still. That's what the enemy, the remote intelligence, wants you to do—to stay still, to acquiesce, to accept the chess board convention. The convention . . . the rules. The situation only exists within the convention, you're only trapped if you believe in the sanctity of the rules. Disobey the rules and you're free.

Because, you see, there's one thing the enemy forgot; and although he's everywhere, it's something he can't possibly change, not now he can't. This isn't just any coach, its a wagon-lit. *Get it?*

It could never work.

It's your only chance, man. You've had your thirty seconds of thinking. Another thirty seconds and you're done for. Your last chance. MOVE.

'I have only one eye,' said Fielding Gray, 'and a face like a broiled lobster. If I appeared on your television programme, old women and children would have fits all over the kingdom.'

'No one is suggesting you should appear,' said Tom Llewyllyn. 'Have you the first idea what this programme is going to be about?'

'No. I don't follow television affairs. There is, thank God, no set at Buttock's Hotel.'

'I'm surprised you're still living there. Now that things are beginning to go your way.'

'Tessie Buttock's been very kind to me,' said Fielding Gray, 'and anyhow I detest change. There's never any change at Buttock's. Even the amount of dirt remains constant: never more, never less.'

Tom Llewyllyn passed a hand through long wavy hair. It was, Fielding noticed, atrociously scurfy. Why didn't Tom's wife Patrica keep him up to scratch? His shoes were filthy, his shirt collar curled up like a piece of damp melba toast, his finger-nails were positively ghoulish. One could only conclude that Patricia liked dirt.

'But fond as you are of Buttock's,' Tom was saying, 'you wouldn't mind a nice little expedition? A temporary change of scene?'

One of the three telephones on his desk rang viciously.

'Llewyllyn,' Tom said into it: 'Today is History.'

While Tom listened patiently to a yakking monologue from the other end, Fielding left his chair and walked to the window, from which he had a bird's eye view of the White City Stadium. How appropriate, he reflected, that the Dog Track should lie almost adjacent to the Television Centre. Both institutions recognisably belonged to the same world— a world, he now told himself, in which he had no business. He was a serious novelist, whereas Television—what was that revolting phrase?—was a popular medium. Being rather vague about his friend's position in the BBC (Tom had hardly been there a week), Fielding had imagined, when invited to call, that they were to discuss the possible dramatisation of one of his novels; but now it appeared that

Tom's new appointment in this palace of nightmares was as Producer of something called 'Today is History', and whatever that phrase might imply it could scarcely comprehend fiction. Well, if Tom wanted his help in broadcasting half-truths to the half-witted, he must look elsewhere.

'I've got him here now,' Tom was saying into the telephone; 'I'll tell him.' He put down the receiver. 'That,' he said to Fielding, 'was the Director of Features. He is an admirer of your work, and he hopes, like me, that you can do something for Today is History.'

'Such as re-writing the nasty bits to reassure your imbecile listeners?'

'Viewers, we call them. Why are you so acid, Fielding?'

'This building, this office, these telephones. This isn't my style, Tom, and I shouldn't have thought it was yours.'

'Then listen. They have given me *carte blanche* to prepare, without censorship or interference, six programmes, each of one hour, about any aspects of contemporary history which I care to choose. Don't say that isn't handsome.'

'You're a writer, even a scholar. Not some kind of cultural whizz-kid.'

'This is 1962, Fielding. This kind of thing is here to stay. It's a challenge which we must face.'

'Don't talk clichés to me, Tom. Save them for your programme.'

Tom's mouth drooped slightly and his eyelids blinked. Why is Fielding so foul to me? he thought. The arrogance of success? But he's not all that successful. Does his face hurt him, his poor ruined face? With an effort Tom said:

'There aren't going to be any clichés in my programme. I've got a large budget and I can afford the best writers. Such as you.' Praise, he thought: writers—a few of them—may be able to resist money, but even the most honest will sell their souls for praise. 'Your last novel,' Tom went on, 'put you in a new class. The first two were merely competent; but *Love's Jest Book* ... as a study in betrayal ... is really memorable.'

'So it ought to be. It all happened, and I was the betrayer.'

'Yes, yes, I know about that,' said Tom soothingly; 'but it doesn't alter the fact that the novel, as it stands, is a very fine piece of work.'

'I don't see how it qualifies me to contribute to your programme.'

'It proves finally and beyond doubt that you can write. Besides,' said Tom, 'I was thinking of another true story of which you have special knowledge.'

'What can you mean?'

'Cyprus. You were there while you were still in the Army.'

'Is that what you meant by a change of scene? I never want to see the filthy place again, Tom. The Cypriots, the Greek ones at any rate—they're the scum of the earth.'

'Who's talking in clichés now?'

'They did this to me,' Fielding hissed, and pointed at his twisted mouth and bright pink grafted face. 'They took one of my eyes and turned the other into a tiny red thing, like a pig's.'

One of the three telephones rang. Tom picked up the wrong receiver, winced, grabbed another at random, turned out lucky.

'I entirely forgot, dear fellow,' said the voice of the Director of Features (creamy, now, and disarming instead of its usual aggressive squawk), 'to tell you what I really rang up for last time. A minor matter of policy. Just as well you should know about it while you're still at the planning stage.'

'I thought I wasn't to be bothered with that,' said Tom, while Fielding slunk away to the window again.

'No more you are, dear fellow. We value your intellectual honesty above everything. But we *should* be most frightfully grateful ... if you *could* just remember ... that *if* you do a programme about—er—people who aren't white ... emergent nations and all that sort of thing ... then it would be very nice if you needn't say anything nasty. If you see what I mean.'

'I am very sympathetic,' said Tom, 'to emergent nations and that sort of thing.'

'No doubt you are'—the creamy voice reverted to the squawk—'but sometimes the facts aren't.'

'Then in such cases,' said Tom firmly, 'one's sympathy has to be qualified.'

'Or'—hopefully—'the facts?'

'You can't qualify facts. You can only establish and state them.'

'You can also assess them in the light of circumstance,' the Director quacked: 'intellectual honesty requires you to.'

19

'If you mention intellectual honesty once more,' said Tom, 'I shall walk out of this building and never come back.'

And be very glad to do so, he thought, as he put down the receiver and looked at the hunched and sulky shoulders by the window. As for Fielding, he thought, why bother with him? Have I not troubles enough? I have taken on this programme as a duty, because I feel that at last I should try to communicate to the people at large something which vitally concerns all of them—the way in which minute by minute history is being made under their noses. I want to tell them about the living process, and then give them true and powerful examples of the process at work; to demonstrate, above all, how very little, in the end, can come of human aspiration and planning, and how very much more results merely from time and chance, which happeneth to us all. This will be a difficult and unpopular message to put over, for it is opposed to all the preconceptions of a society which takes for granted that in this world, man is king. Although I myself am a socialist, dedicated to the progress and betterment of mankind (insofar as these are possible), I am to advance a philosophy of pessimism which will be ill-received at best and the only justification of which must be that it is true. To tell the truth is hard enough, even when one is promised *carte blanche*; and there are already signs that the promise is not wholly sincere ... for whenever people start talking about 'intellectual honesty', one must reach for a lie-detector. With all this and much more to worry about, Tom thought, I should indeed be happy to quit this Tower of Babel and go straight back to writing my books. But if for the time, at least, I feel myself committed to stay here and try my best, one thing I can do to make life easier is not to employ tiresome and reactionary paranoiacs like Fielding Gray. There are plenty of other people, after all, who would be only too glad to be brought in.

So Tom Llewyllyn spoke within his heart, and then jutted his chin furiously at the obstinate back by the window. But even as he did so, he knew that he would persevere with Fielding, and this for two reasons. First, Fielding was one of the few able young writers in England who would understand and sympathise with the unfashionable thesis which Tom wished to put over; and secondly, Fielding was an old friend who could certainly use the money. He could not,

Tom knew, be making much from the sale of his novels, despite their success of esteem, and although he also reviewed books, this would bring in peanuts. There was no risk of Fielding's being starved or cruelly pressed, but he had been in London for three years now, unable ever to quit it for more than a very few days, and for the sake of his health and his writing he needed a proper change.

And so now:

'The money will be very good,' said Tom to the back at the window.

'Nothing can be very good after what happened to me in Cyprus,' Fielding said without turning.

'It could even be,' said Tom wearily, 'that you might get a bit of your own back.'

'How? By throwing bombs about like they did?'

'That's over now. There's peace. A truce, at any rate.'

'So there was when they did this to me. An agreed truce of two hours while the bodies were being cleared up. And right in the middle of it ... I tell you those people are scum.'

'Then get your own back by proving it. That's why I want you to go there. The trouble's over now but there's more coming, because there are forces at work which have not been brought under proper control. The lull at the moment is only temporary because the Greek Cypriots are still up to something—something very unpleasant, by the smell of it. If you can prove to the world—and I mean *prove*, Fielding—that they're not the sturdy freedom-lovers of liberal legend but just a pack of cruel and treacherous bastards, then you'll have got a bit of your own back.'

'More likely I'll just get the other eye blown out,' said Fielding, still without turning.

There was a knock on the door, which was then opened, before invitation could be given, by a stringy young woman with a put-upon face and a sluttish cardigan.

'Miss Enid Jackson,' she said; 'from Administration.'

'Yes, Miss Jackson?'

'You know why I'm here.'

'I'm afraid not.'

'Yes, you do. Your National Insurance Card. I've rung you several times. Now you're employed here we have to have your National Insurance Card.'

'Yes, yes, I know,' said Tom. 'I'll stamp the thing myself.

'At home.'

'You seem to have very rough and ready ideas about social administration, Mr Llewyllyn. It is your employers' responsibility to st——'

'—And I've just told you I'll do it for them.'

'You can't,' said Miss Jackson with prim satisfaction. 'I must say, if everyone was as ignorant about welfare procedures as you appear to be——'

'—Look, sweetheart,' said Tom, stalking round his desk at Enid Jackson, 'I've been a bloody socialist all my life and I don't need you to lecture me on welfare. But I've always been working on my own till now, and if ever I had one of those footling cards I've certainly lost it. So be a good girl, will you, and rustle me up another.'

'I'm afraid it's not as easy as that. Either you must produce a card fully stamped up to March the twenty-second, which is the day you joined this Corporation, or you must furnish me with a full explanation as to why it is not available.'

'One or the other you shall have, sweetheart. I promise. But not just this minute ... please.'

'Very well. But I should add that until the position has been regularised your employment here is not on a satisfactory official basis. Good morning ... Mr Llewyllyn.'

Tom went back to his desk and put both hands through his hair. Huge flakes of dandruff fell, like ashes from a bonfire.

'Help me, Fielding,' said Tom in a small voice. 'It's so strange here. I didn't want to come and I hate it. Help me. Don't refuse to be on my side now I've asked you.'

At long last Fielding turned from the window and smiled his grotesque smile.

'If you put it like that, my dear,' he said: 'after Miss Enid Jackson, I can hardly refuse.'

'So when will you be off, dear?' said Tessie Buttock that evening in Buttock's Hotel.

'Two or three days,' said Fielding; 'Tom's very urgent. But what I can't understand is what he expects me to discover. The trouble in Cyprus is over. They've got their independence, and that must surely be an end of it.'

'But we've still got soldiers there?'

'Only in agreed bases on the south-coast—for which we

pay a whacking great rent. They can hardly start trouble about that.'

'You trust naughty Tom, dear. He's got a nose for dirt.' She scooped up Albert Edward, the hotel dog, who was glumly peeing on the sofa, and settled him in her lap. 'Woozums, woozums,' she cawed: 'woozums remember naughty Tom? He was a bit vague about money,' she said to Fielding, 'but when he did anything he always had a very clear reason. He must have a reason for sending you off like this, and I don't doubt he told you.'

'Yes,' said Fielding, remembering what Tom had said after the departure of Enid Jackson; 'but I'm not convinced.'

'Tell us, dear, anyway. Albert Edward needs his mind taking off his poor old bladder.'

'Well, he started by looking back a bit. He said that Colonel Grivas devised a terrorist strategy—chucking bombs at civilians and so on—because he couldn't hope to win on a straightforward confrontation. He just hadn't the weapons or the men. But even so, Tom said, Grivas was a brave man with a fine war record, and it must have gone against his nature to play it so dirty. By instinct and upbringing he was a soldier and not an assassin.'

'Nasty little runt he always looked in the papers.'

'But nevertheless a fighter—as the Germans found out in the forties. So Tom's theory is that he didn't want to adopt terrorist methods—or at any rate not against unarmed civilians—but in the end was persuaded into it.'

'I'm not one to speak against Tom,' Tessie said, 'but if you ask me, all you need do is look at that Grivas's face in his photos and you've got all the explanation you need. We wouldn't have him staying in our hotel, would we, woozums?'

'I agree with you, Tessie. But *if* Tom is right—and he's been right before about this kind of thing—then we're left with an interesting question.'

'You mean, who talked the little bugger into it?'

'Right. And where did he come from to do the talking?'

'Russia,' said Tessie, for whom all evils had only one source: 'bloody reds, wanting us done out of our empire.'

'The reds aren't the only people, Tessie, who want us done out of our empire. But leave that on one side, whoever *did* persuade Grivas (on Tom's theory) may still be around getting ready to do some more persuading. There are a lot of young Cypriots who tasted blood in the last affair, and once young men have tasted blood they're bored by the idea of going back to be peasants—or even pimps, which in Cyprus is the only alternative. Which leaves them nothing to do except sharpen their knives and listen to anyone who wants to stir up trouble.'

'Like the Russians,' said Tessie, unshakeable.

'As to that,' said Fielding, 'we shall see. But I still think the whole thing's just been thought up out of nothing by Tom.'

'So,' said plump, kind Maisie in her Shepherd's Market flat, 'this is the last time before you go off?'

''Fraid so, Maisie,' said Fielding: 'let's make it nice and slow, to remember.'

'It's you that's always so quick, duckie. Try the nineteen times table. They say it helps you to hold it back.'

'Nineteen ... Thirty-eight ... Fifty-seven ... Sorry, Maisie, it's no good...'

'Never mind, dearie. You can have that one on the house. Just get your breath back first, then have a look at these pictures, and we can do it again when you're ready.'

'No one else coming?'

'Not for an hour or so. And the fact is, lovie, I want to tell you something. You've been coming here—how long is it now?——'

'—Three years——'

'—So we're old friends, really, and now that you're going away for a bit, I want to tell you something before you go.'

Maisie waddled comfortably to the wardrobe and came back with a split of champagne and two glasses.

'This is on the house too,' she said, 'just this once. Now tell me, Fielding Gray: this Cyprus business—is it dangerous?'

Whenever Maisie called him 'Fielding' or 'Fielding Gray' instead of 'dearie' or 'lovie', he knew there was something unusual coming. So now he put aside the photographs and gave Maisie his best attention.

'Dangerous?' he said. 'Why should you ask that? I thought you were going to tell me something.'

Maisie scratched her naked bottom and plonked it down beside him on the bed.

'Dangerous or not,' she said, 'you're going to Cyprus to try and dig up dirt. Which means that there's a certain kind of person you'll be dealing with. Always the same kind when there's dirt to be buried or dug up again, and I know that kind, because I had a lot of 'em in and out of this flat some years back, using it as a post office for that racket of Salvadori's. And what I found out, Fielding Gray, was this: they're poison all right, but they can't do you much harm provided you remember just one rule, which is what I'm going to tell you now.'

She paused, took a gulp of champagne and fiddled briefly with his hair.

'One rule, Maisie? Only one?'

'Only one. Don't let them know anything at all about the *real* you.'

'As if I would.' What a miserable mouse, he thought, this mountain has brought forth.

'But you do, darling, you do all the time. We all do, unless we're on our guard. Even if you just go to a restaurant with someone, at the end of an hour they know what you like to eat and drink—something about the real you. Not very important, but something. I know something much more important: what you're like when you do ... this.' She tweaked him gently. 'It's safe with me, but *their* kind 'ud use it all right if they knew. And there are more important things still—the things in *here*.' She held two pudgy hands over her embosomed heart. 'If you let them know what you've got in here, Fielding Gray, they'll have you cold.'

'But why should I let them know?'

'Because it's always coming out without us noticing ... in front of people we think we can trust. And the next thing you know it comes whirring back at you like a bloody boomerang and slices off your nut. So you make sure, Fielding Gray, that what you've got in there'—she traced a little circle round his left nipple with her finger-nail—'stays there good and tight. Promise?'

'I promise. Thank you, Maisie.'

'That's my good boy. Now you drink up that fizz, and have a look at those nice pictures, and in no time at all you'll be feeling like the Albert Memorial.'

Gregory Stern, who was Fielding's publisher and also

Tom's, brought his wife Isobel, who was the younger sister of Tom's wife Patricia, to see Fielding off at Victoria Station.

'All I can say,' Stern said, 'is that this is a mistake. You've let yourself be soft-soaped into this nonsense of Tom's instead of staying responsibly at home and writing your next novel for me.'

'Don't be such a boring old Jew,' said Isobel: 'you're only jealous because Tom's paying him so much more than you can.'

'Gadding about in Cyprus,' grumbled Stern, 'thinking you're Paddy Leigh Fermor. You're old enough to know better.'

'It's only for a short time,' said Fielding, anxious to re-assure Stern, who for three years now had been a generous publisher and a loyal friend.

'A short time, he says.' Gregory Stern turned his eyes up to the roof and ran his fingers over his waistcoat buttons as though he were typing a letter of complaint on them. 'A short time. So why are you going by the train, which is three days to Athens, instead of by the aeroplane, which is three hours?'

Since his marriage to Isobel the hitherto impeccably Etonian Stern had tended more and more to adopt a Yiddish idiom. This he did, in Fielding's view, in order to annoy his wife and make her unkind to him; for Gregory was something of a masochist (they said) and enjoyed being bullied.

'That's right,' Isobel said now, inflating her huge breasts at Gregory and hopping from one thin leg to the other: 'go and poke your snout into everyone else's business. Why shouldn't he go by train if he wants to?'

'It's just that I like trains,' Fielding said to Gregory, 'and if you'll excuse me, I think it's time I got on this one.'

'No hurry, my dear. I've got something for you.'

Unnoticed by Isobel, who was now busy leering at a sailor, Gregory drew Fielding on one side.

'For luck,' Gregory said. He produced a cylindrical metal case about an inch long and one-quarter of an inch in diameter at the ends, from one of which he now prised out a tiny roll of parchment. 'We call it a Mezuzah,' he explained: 'on one side is written a text, on the other the divine name, Shaddai. The case with the parchment inside it must be fastened to the outer door of a man's house. But if he travels, why should he not take one with him?'

He re-inserted the roll and handed the little tube to Fielding.

'Thank you very much, Gregory,' said Fielding, touched. 'But why should you think I need luck?'

'Don't we all, my dear?'

'Yes. But you've made this somehow special.'

'You are special to me, Fielding Gray. I want you back in one piece to write more novels.'

'That sailor's a pansy,' Isobel said: 'he isn't taking any notice of me.'

'So he isn't taking any notice. So he doesn't like fat breasts and thin legs,' said Gregory. And then to Fielding, 'But why *are* you taking the train? They're very boring these days, you know. No one uses them, so there aren't any more madonnas of the sleeping-cars or anything jolly like that.'

'Precisely. I shall have three days of entire privacy. No one, no one at all, can get at me or ring me up or dun me or make demands. I shall be sealed off in a travelling womb, without guilt or responsibility of any kind.'

'I wish I could come with you,' said Isobel, 'and be a madonna of a sleeping-car.'

A door was slammed by mistake farther down the platform, and a group of Americans flew into a screeching panic. In the midst of them one face suddenly stood out: a face like Mr Punch's, with a chin that curved up to meet the tip of a long, hooked nose, this being surmounted by spectacles which were glinting, from fifty yards away, straight into Fielding's eyes. I've seen that face before, he thought. It knows me and I know it. What's more, it's watching me. Who? Why? Where have I seen it before?

'Anything the matter, my dear?'

'No ...'

'Then don't forget to go and see Detterling as you pass through Athens. I wired him and he'll be expecting you ... Are you listening, Fielding? I was saying about Detterling——'

'——Yes, yes, I heard. Any messages?'

The spectacles had gone now. One moment they had been there, glinting straight at him. He had turned his head, only for a second, in response to Stern's insistence, and now that he had turned back they were gone. Where their owner had been, there were simply two wailing women, still under the impression that they were being treacherously left behind by the train, savagely jostling each other to get through a door.

'... And tell Detterling,' Gregory was saying, 'not to worry about the Cavafy memoirs. I haven't yet found a translator, and anyhow I'm already doing too many bugger books this year.'

More doors slammed, this time in earnest. Fielding backed towards the train. He didn't offer to kiss Isobel, though he had known her well for some time now, but she darted on to him and landed a great splosh on his little twisted mouth. Gregory looked on benignly, then himself came forward to kiss Fielding's cheek.

'God bless you, my dear. Keep the Mezuzah carefully.'

'Of course, Gregory ... I nearly forgot—where's Detterling staying?'

'The Grande Bretagne. I ask you. The firm is paying, so he stays at the Grande Bretagne.'

'He would have done anyway,' said Isobel; 'and you're just a dreary, cheese-paring yid.'

Gregory blushed so much with pleasure that his scarlet face shone as clear as a traffic lamp on the platform until the first bend chopped it from sight.

2: En Route

The man with the spectacles made himself known at Munich.

Fielding had seen nothing of him on the boat from Dover to Ostend, nor at dinner in the restaurant-car that evening, nor at breakfast the following morning. But just as the train was moving out of Munich, and as Fielding was walking along the Athens coach on his way to lunch, a figure advanced at him down the corridor, jutting its upturned chin and flashing its glasses like morse lamps.

'I was just coming,' the figure said, 'to suggest you joined me for a spot of food.'

The figure put up a hand to smooth the very scant hair above its deep and pallid forehead, a precise yet nugatory gesture which at once prompted Fielding's memory.

'Percival,' he said, 'Leonard Percival. Göttingen, 1952. Wessex Fusiliers.'

'I'm flattered,' said Percival, 'to be so accurately documented. Members of humble line regiments are easily forgotten.'

'But you weren't, as it turned out, quite what you seemed at the time.'

'Neither were you. Who would have thought that the pampered and pouting captain of Earl Hamilton's Light Dragoons would turn into a distinguished novelist?'

'Not distinguished yet,' said Fielding, smug nevertheless.

'You might be if you stick to it. And if you don't waste time,' Percival said, lightly but very clearly, 'meddling with what doesn't concern you. Come on, we're blocking the corridor.'

They walked through to the restaurant-car, where Percival ordered the cheapest menu at five Marks and Fielding the most expensive at fifteen, along with a bottle of Spätburgunder Walporzeim 1951.

'Always the best of everything,' said Percival, 'for Earl Hamilton's Light Dragoons. The gastronomic menu, the priciest wine on the list—and travelling by wagon-lit, but of course. A compartment to yourself, the attendant tells me.'

'The BBC's paying.' Fielding looked at Percival's exquisitely cut suit and manicured nails. '*You* don't look exactly ground down, come to that.'

'I'm just mean,' said Percival slyly. 'I travel second class to save money ... and because I know my place as an ex-officer of one of the dowdier regiments.'

'For God's sake stop harping on the Army. I've been out for over three years. And you were never really in it. You were a spy in Fusilier's clothing. Still spying ... Leonard?'

Percival said nothing while he was served with consommé and Fielding with crayfish in mayonnaise. Then:

'I still retain the knack,' Percival said.

'The knack of hanging around sleeping-car attendants scrounging for information?'

'Paying for it. That's why I can only afford the cheapest lunch.'

'It surely can't have cost much just to learn that I had a compartment to myself.'

'Five Marks,' said Percival severely; 'or the equivalent of one good-size glass of that Spätburgunder Walporzeim.'

'Then allow me to recompense you,' said Fielding, pouring for them both from the bottle, 'and also to enquire why you were so keen to find out. Are you hoping that I shall invite you to move into the upper bunk?'

The waiter thumped down a debased Hamburger in front of Percival and obsequiously presented Fielding with a veal steak smothered in cream on a lordly silver dish. When the subsequent ceremonies were concluded, Percival said:

'As it happens, you could do a lot worse. For the whole point is, Major Fielding Gray, that an empty bunk can be filled. Anywhere between here and Athens.'

'Not if I've booked the entire compartment.'

'The attendant, as we already know, is venal. If he supported the interloper, pleading, let us say, some obscure regulation about the priorities of travellers on official business, you'd be done for, wouldn't you?'

'It would be disagreeable, certainly.'

'Very disagreeable, I should say, if your companion suddenly pointed a long knife at you in the middle of the night and started asking rude questions about your interest in Cyprus.'

Although this picture was melodramatic and absurd, there was a grating quality in Percival's voice which compelled Fielding to take him seriously.

'Why on earth should he behave like that?'

'Because,' said Percival patiently, 'his standard of manners would not be that of Earl Hamilton's Light Dragoons and he would be eager to have your answer.'

'Which would be that I'm going to get material for a television programme on how the gallant Cypriots achieved independence and what they propose to do with it.'

'As you very well know,' said Percival, 'neither topic will bear much examination. I think—don't you?—that your hypothetical bedfellow would want more convincing proof of your good will.'

'Such as?'

'An immediate readiness to get off this comfortable train

and take one going the other way. Quite unthinkable, of course: one doesn't take orders from foreigners.'

Fielding crossly waved away a rich pudding, which Percival re-captured from the waiter.

'I'll have some more of that Spätburgunder, if you don't mind,' Percival said, and poured a brimming glass.

'Is any of this in the least likely to happen?'

'That's just what I was spending all those Deutschmarks to find out. Were you to be alone, I enquired of the attendant, for the whole journey?'

'And was I?'

'Of course. The English gentleman had booked the whole compartment. The expected, the inevitable answer.'

'Then why pay five Deutschmarks for it?'

'To observe the way in which it was made. Very much too glib. Not reassuring, I'm afraid.'

Fielding hesitated before answering. He had last seen Leonard Percival ten years ago, when they were both serving, though in very different capacities, in the same barracks at Göttingen. What little he had then known of Percival he had not much liked, and it had subsequently appeared that Percival had been playing a discreditable role in a discreditable business. Nevertheless, that business had had official sanction at a high level, and there was no reason at all to doubt Percival's professional competence or (if one allowed for the obliquity which that profession involved) his present good faith. That Percival's motives were devious and, ultimately, quite unconcerned with Fielding's welfare was probable; but here and now, if Percival was warning him, he would do well to listen.

'All right,' Fielding said: 'then why not move in with me? That should settle any nonsense. I'm told that I snore rather badly, but even so a free bed for two nights should appeal to your sense of economy.'

'A charming offer. But unfortunately I'm not much loved in Yugoslavia, so I must leave the train in Austria this afternoon. A pity: we could have talked about the dear old days in BAOR.'

It was a measure of the ascendancy which Percival had obtained over Fielding during their conversation that Fielding, faced with this unexpected news, felt suddenly and totally vulnerable. Although the dining-car was grossly overheated, he found himself shivering as if he had been stripped to the skin.

'But ... what shall I do?'

'Do, my dear fellow? Read your books. Look out of the window. Eat delicious meals ... the restaurant-car which comes on at the Yugoslav frontier, by the way, is the best on this trip—or so I used to think when I was still allowed in it. The regime considers it a good advertisement, you see.'

'Leonard. If, as you suggest, someone tries ... to get at me ... what shall I do?'

'Keep a stiff upper lip, old chap, and remember the honour of the regiment.'

'*Leonard*——'

'—Don't tell me that an officer of Lord Hamilton's Horse is getting into a funk.'

'I simply,' said Fielding, pulling himself together, 'want to know what course of action you recommend.'

'Very simple. Tomorrow evening you will have a choice. Either you can eat an early dinner, at about six o'clock, in the Yugoslav dining-car before reaching the Greek frontier; or you can eat later on in the Greek car, which will be put on at the frontier station. Which will you choose?'

'The Greek one. I hate dining too early.'

'You just don't listen, do you? I have already told you that the Yugoslav dining-car provides the best meals on this whole run. Take my tip, Major Gray: do you stomach ... and yourself ... a favour.'

Percival rose to his feet.

'Ten per cent for service, isn't it?' he asked.

'You should know. You're so familiar with this line.'

Percival counted five Marks and fifty Pfennigs, checked them carefully and put them on the table.

'The Greeks charge ten per cent too,' he said, 'and the Yugoslavs fifteen. But you're not the man to bother yourself about an extra five per cent, now are you?'

Smiling, Percival backed away down the aisle and raised a hand in farewell.

'Anyway,' he said, 'it's being paid by the BBC.'

As Fielding re-entered his compartment after lunch, a face rose to meet him: his own. It was a clear second before he recognised himself in the looking glass over the hand-basin, and during that second a thick sweat of fear gathered in his groin. He had failed to know himself, as he realised when he was calmer, because Leonard Percival was still so much the same that he, Fielding, had been carried back in time and had forgotten, if only for a few moments, how he himself had changed. The face he had expected to see in the mirror was that of ten years ago: clear eyes widely set, Greek nose, voluptuous mouth and becomingly cleft chin. Now all that remained from that time was his hair, still thick and glowing auburn, better, he thought, than Percival can show or ever could. He stroked it fondly with both hands, watching them in the glass; my beautiful hair, he thought. And then, what shall I do? I'm already starting at my own shadow; what shall I do if ever the threat is real?

The trouble was, he thought, as he sat down by the window, that Percival's communication was on the one hand (if one thought about it properly for two seconds together) wildly improbable and yet on the other hand so authoritative. Its authority it derived from something in Percival's manner which had procured him Fielding's respect; and however laughable, however inconsistent what Percival actually said, Fielding felt somehow compelled to puzzle at it until it made sense. It was like being faced with a corrupt passage in a classical author: the words, as they stood, might be gibberish, but since they had been written by a great man there must be some way of emending and construing them so that their message would at last become clear.

What, then, had Percival been trying to say? And why couldn't he have come straight out with it? Even his manner, although it had won Fielding's reluctant attention, had been ambiguous. Perhaps he had been spying for so long that he was now incapable of doing anything directly: an occupational debility like tennis elbow or housemaid's knee. But this was no time for random speculation. Analyse: what had Percival said and what did he mean?

If one ignored the jokes about money and class, what it seemed to amount to was a series of warnings, each of a nature—and here was the confusion—to invalidate the one which preceded it. Percival had started by warning him off the whole project: stick to your work, he had said; don't meddle with what doesn't concern you. Having thus expressed his disapproval, however, Percival had then gone on to offer assistance or at any rate advice on the plain assumption that Fielding would see the journey through ('one doesn't take orders from foreigners'). He had told Fielding to be on his guard against a possible intruder, who might corner him in his compartment, with the connivance of the wagon-lit attendant, and start asking awkward questions. Leave aside the vagueness of all this (who would the intruder be? where and what his nation?), leave aside its sheer implausibility, one then came to the biggest *non sequitur* of all. For when asked what action should be taken to deal with the mysterious stranger, Percival had merely told him to dine, on the evening of the next day, not in the Greek restaurant-car but in the Yugoslav one. Percival evidently regarded this as a simple and obvious precaution, but how it could help to thwart malicious intruders from getting into one's sleeping compartment was more than Fielding could compute.

Outside his window, April sparkled among the passing pine-trees. A stretch of lake, a village with church and tower, onion-topped, a green field with cows. Another stretch of lake, another village with church, another field ... As the countryside unrolled strictly repetitive like the background to an early Disney cartoon, Fielding's head began to nod forward. Who had sent Leonard and why? Would he turn up later, or did his assignment end when he left the train in Austria? Where in Austria? If only Leonard had been more plain ... but here he was in the compartment, now was Fielding's chance to get things straight. 'Tell me, Leonard...' But Leonard wasn't listening; he was looking into the mirror, stroking his hair, which had grown thick and curly and auburn, just like Fielding's. 'Do you like my hair?' Leonard said. 'I've been using an expensive new lotion—rather presumptuous in a member of the middle class, but then I was envious of yours. Why should you Dragoons always have the best?' He turned to face Fielding, and he had Fielding's face as well as his hair, Fielding's face as it had been ten years ago, in Göttingen, where the sun sparkled among the pine-trees in the spring. 'I love you,' said Leonard-Fielding, the ghost-Fielding from Göttingen, 'I love you so much, please give me a kiss.' But Fielding knew that it was dangerous to be kissed by ghosts and he shrank up against the window, while the ghost-Fielding held out his arms and smiled wider and wider, obscenely inviting, a living corpse cackling with laughter, its

34

face splitting into great sores of PUS PUS PUS, red and yellow like a Turner sunset, POX POX POX.

Fielding woke to the heavy knocking on the door.

'No,' he screamed, 'no.'

The door was flung open and a huge man thrust himself through the narrow entrance.

'Gruss Gott, mein Herr,' said the man reproachfully: 'Austrian customs, please.'

Tom Llewyllyn and his wife Patricia lived in an angular flat in Southwell Gardens. At about the time Fielding's train passed over the German–Austrian frontier, Tom returned home from the Television Centre, sat down in front of the gas-fire, and said:

'Is the water hot? I need a bath.'

But Patricia had forgotten to turn on the immersion heater.

'It's hardly tea-time yet,' she wailed.

'I couldn't bear that place a second longer. Anyhow, I *have* asked you always to turn it on by three. Just to make sure.'

But Patricia had been out shopping, she explained, and she had had to take Baby, their two-year-old daughter, to the dentist, and she had been distracted later by a long telephone call from her sister, Isobel Stern.

'What was Isobel on about?'

'She and Gregory went to see Fielding off at Victoria yesterday.'

Patricia hesitated, then picked Baby off the filthy carpet and began to change her nappies.

'It can't,' said Tom, 'have taken Isobel very long to tell you that.'

'She'd had ... one of her feelings.'

Tom shrugged.

'Fine. Isobel's had one of her feelings and there's no hot water. And another thing,' he said: 'when you change that child you ought to wash and powder her.'

Patricia, who before her marriage in 1959 had kept house immaculately for her father, Sir Edwin Turbot, and had been remarkable for strength of character, had changed in the last three years. She had become sluttish and inefficient. Tom thought that this was the result of her strong attachment to Sir Edwin, who from being a prominent statesman was now rapidly going ga-ga: Patricia, that was to say, was declining in her behaviour out of an unconscious wish to share the old man's predicament. In which case, Tom could only hope that Sir Edwin would very soon die and so release Patricia from the need to emulate him; though of course it might work the other way—Patricia might develop an unconscious wish to share his coffin. Tom sighed heavily. It was all too complicated, would indeed have been insupportable had he not loved her very much.

Meanwhile Patricia had clumped reluctantly away to the bathroom with Baby and was now clumping back.

'No hot water, of course,' she said, 'so I couldn't wash her. But,' with an air of pride, 'I've turned on the immersion heater.'

Baby began to dribble on Patricia's lap.

'That child smells,' said Tom.

'That was what Isobel said,' remarked Patricia impenitently, 'about Fielding Gray.'

'Rubbish. There isn't a more fastidious man in England.'

'Not literally. It was all part of Isobel's feeling. There was, she said, a smell of death.'

'She's just dramatising as usual.'

All the same, Tom thought, I wish this hadn't come so soon after what I heard this morning. For that morning he had been visited by a man from the BBC department which handled sound-broadcasting in the Near East. He had heard, the man said, that Tom was sending a man to think up a programme about Cyprus. While it was no affair of his, and he did hope Tom wouldn't think he was interfering, he felt he ought to say that the time was ... ill chosen. Why, Tom had replied: there was no sign of present trouble, and if trouble should suddenly come, so much the more interesting for his writer on the spot. It wasn't as simple as that, the man observed: there wasn't going to be any trouble—not for some time—but there were—*sensitivities*. In that case, could not the Cypriots have given the BBC a polite but firm warning to stay away for the time being? It wasn't so much the Cypriots who were being sensitive, the man said, as ... somebody else. Who and why? It was impolitic, the man opined, to ask such crude and direct questions about so very sensitive an area; after which cryptic pronouncement he had glided out of Tom's office.

Tom wondered now whether to tell Patricia about this and decided against it. She would only say that it confirmed Isobel's 'feeling'; and since Tom, despite himself, was inclined to think the same, and was therefore furious with himself for being so weak and irrational, further discussion of the topic could only lead to loss of temper. Isobel, he told himself sternly, was a silly little ass, and the Near East man was a pretentious little ass, and best leave it at that.

'Isobel has too little to do,' he said now: 'why doesn't she have a baby?'

'They're trying very hard. Gregory wants one even more than she does.'

'A baby,' said Tom, looking with fond disgust at the drooling child on Patricia's lap, 'should be enough to settle even her. Smell of death, indeed. The next thing we know she'll have brought a crystal ball.'

'Once,' said Patricia, 'when we were children, she organised a seance.'

'What happened?'

'Nothing really,' Patricia said. 'She pretended to go into a trance and shouted a lot of rude words. She claimed afterwards she'd never heard them before, but she was always hanging round the gardener's boy, so I expect she learnt them from him.'

As the afternoon retreated from his window and the evening filtered slowly among the pine trees, Fielding alternately pondered and dozed. Most times that he fell asleep he was woken abruptly after a few minutes by acid heartburn which resulted from his gastronomic lunch. Once, however, he slept longer and was roused only by a tapping on the glass beside his head. This turned out to be Percival, who was standing on a platform and grinning. As soon as he saw Fielding was awake, Percival pushed his canines down over his lower lip in a rather good imitation of Count Dracula, waved, turned on his heel, and walked off with a swirl of his stylish overcoat towards the exit from the station, which, Fielding now saw, was called Linz. Apparently Percival had no luggage; nor, Fielding reflected, would one expect him to have any; like all vampires he doubtless travelled light.

Although Fielding's thoughts grew no clearer as the evening went on, by the end of dinner he had reached a decision. The meal, being Austrian, was poor and his appetite even poorer; but two whiskies and a bottle of brisk red wine helped him to formulate his plan with some confidence. Not that it needed much formulation, for it was extremely simple: he would just follow Percival's advice and see what came of it. He would stay awake, which should not be difficult after his comatose afternoon, until, in a few hours, the train crossed from Austria into Yugoslavia; he would then lock the door of his compartment and go to bed, fully dressed in case of night alarums; and for the rest, he would keep his one eye cocked the next day and in the evening would take great care, as Percival had urged, to dine early in the Yugoslav restaurant-car and eschew the Greek. Percival had assured him that this was the way to evade the danger that threatened; and though Percival's logic was obscure, the situation was Percival's production, so to speak, and Percival must be allowed to know best.

Having finally settled this over three large glasses of brandy, Fielding purchased a bottle of the same from the steward and went back to his compartment, where he amused himself (as he often did when slightly drunk) with reading his favourite passages from his own books.

When the train reached the Yugoslav frontier, there was less shouting and shunting than there had been at any frontier previous. Although Fielding had expected much activity from officials, these merely glanced at the pile of passports held by the wagon-lit attendant for his charges and passed on down the train.

Through his window, Fielding watched the Austrian dining-car as it was rolled away down a side-line (good riddance) and the Yugoslav one which was being moved up in its place. Now what, he thought to himself, can be so special about *that*, that Percival should have been at such pains to recommend it? No answer suggested itself, so he stretched himself flat on his bunk, half-anaesthetised with brandy, to sleep.

'Do you think,' said Tom Llewyllyn at breakfast, 'that we might have kippers occasionally instead of boiled eggs?'

'Baby can't eat kippers,' Patricia said.

'Baby could have her boiled egg and *we* could have kippers.'

'Then Baby would be jealous.'

'Not if she can't eat kippers anyway.'

'She doesn't *know* she can't eat them anyway.'

Baby squirted half a boiled egg, carefully accumulated in her ample cheeks, on to Tom's dark suit.

'Oh dear,' said Patricia. Her dressing gown fell apart to reveal the insides of two long, snaky breasts.

'Never mind,' said Tom, breathing heavily, 'I'll go to Shepherd's Bush in the check one.'

'Oh, darling ... I'm afraid I forgot ... It's still at the cleaners. But I expect a sports coat and flannels will be all right. I mean, for the *BBC* ...'

'It just so happens that I'm having lunch with the Director of Features.'

'Are you?' said Patricia, unimpressed. 'Well, eat as much as you can, darling, because I've got to take Baby to the clinic and I'll be too tired to cook proper dinner.'

Fielding had his breakfast in the Yugoslav restaurant-car. The head waiter, although he looked and moved like a retired wrestler, had a very graceful address.

'Eggs and bacon,' he said, 'for an English.'

Fielding, whose liver felt like a badly blown up football on a muddy day, politely demurred; but when the head waiter's face started to crumple, he nodded assent after all and was served a few minutes later, with the best plate of eggs and bacon he had eaten in several months.

Gregory and Isobel Stern always had breakfast downstairs in the dining-room, fully dressed. It made, as Gregory put it, a crisp start to the day; and since they lived in Chelsea, where there was much laxity in the air, it was important to have as many crisp habits as possible.

Gregory ate some patent breakfast food compound of ground-nuts and sawdust, while Isobel knocked into a great plate of kedgeree, which she had cooked for herself.

'What are you doing today?' Gregory asked.

'Spring cleaning. What are *you* doing? Sitting in that office trying to cheat your authors, I suppose.'

It was said with the malicious affection which of all her qualities Gregory loved most.

'I'm going to read some of the stuff which Detterling's been sending from Athens.'

'That reminds me,' Isobel said: 'you know I told you I

had that ... feeling ... about Fielding Gray?'

'Yes'—embarrassed and uneasy.

'Well, I had another last night in a dream. Fielding and I were looking at some old ruin somewhere. All I can remember is a large stone doorway, square and flat, with two animals carved above it, large dogs they looked like, sniffing up at a pillar. There was this same feeling of death I had at the station, only much stronger, as though the whole place was kind of ... seeped in it.'

'Steeped in it,' Gregory said.

'Well, there was a sort of *ooze*. That's seeping, isn't it?'

'But the verb is intransitive and so cannot be used in the passive voice.'

'Passive yourself, you old cow. But the thing was,' Isobel went on, 'that there was another feeling too. With all that death about, Fielding was somehow enormously happy, quite radiant with it. "It hasn't been like this for seventeen years," he said.'

'Seventeen?'

'Yes, wasn't it odd? If he'd said fifteen or twenty it would have seemed quite natural; but seventeen—so precise. That's why I remembered it.'

Gregory champed his breakfast food.

'What was Fielding so happy about?' he enquired.

'The dream ended then. After Fielding spoke I saw a sort of blue flash a long way off ... and then the dream ended.'

Gregory worked hard with his tongue to remove the coating of slush from his palate. The stuff might have been made of acorns. Why was it supposed to be so good for him?

'Could it have been the sea, this blue flash?' he asked.

'P'raps. Why?'

'Just a thought. You've never been to Greece, have you?'

'No. Why?'

'Just another thought. Tell me. Isobel my wife: what for must I eat this rubbish every morning?'

His eyes entreated.

'Because you're a weedy old Jew and it's good for you.'

Gregory chuckled.

'So I'm a weedy old Jew who must go now to work for my shekels. Will my wife be waiting this evening?'

'Waiting and ready,' she said.

The Yugoslav countryside was green, rolling and interminable. During the morning Fielding read Richardson's *Clarissa*, which was even more interminable, and for lunch he has a glass of light beer and a piece of delicious but unnamed fish.

'Will the English not eat more?' the head waiter pleaded. 'Our food is good, yes?'

'Your food is excellent. But I'm saving myself up for dinner.'

Fielding pointed to a printed slip on the table, which begged to inform passengers in French, English, German and Italian (but not in Serbo-Croat) that dinner would be at 6.30 p.m. in order to enable them to conclude the meal in comfort before the train reached the Greek frontier.

'Ah, yes,' said the head waiter, and ambled crab-wise away down the aisle.

'Fielding Gray, good,' the Director of Features said: 'Cyprus ... not so good.'

'Fielding knows about Cyprus,' said Tom.

'And other places, I take it.' The Director looked sternly at Tom's tweed jacket. 'So why Cyprus?' he said.

'Why not? I told you I was sending him there some days ago. Why bring it up again now?'

The Director, being of privileged rank, was lunching Tom in a private room in the Television Centre. A vegetarian, he had ordered the meal in advance: an undressed salad with some faddy kind of bread and for Tom, as a concession, a hard-boiled egg.

'What's your ... line on Cyprus?' the Director of Features asked.

'That depends on Fielding. I've suggested he should start by checking back in the record for ... inconsistencies.'

The Director shuddered.

'Cyprus is an emergent nation now, you know that.'

'No more so now than it was a week ago—when I first told you I was sending Gray. If you've got any new objections to his assignment, for God's sake be plain.'

'When will he reach Athens?'

'In about twenty-four hours. Rather less.'

'Send him a wire there,' the Director quacked. 'Tell him to hang on in Athens until further notice, as you may want him to research into something different after all.'

'Is this what's known as *carte blanche*?'

'Simply a suggestion,' said the Director, suddenly very mild, 'which may be in everyone's best interest. Just ask him to wait. He'll probably be glad of a chance to have a good look round Athens.'

'That's not the point, Director.'

'I'm only trying to insure against ... muddle. And that rings a bell. There've been complaints from Administration that you haven't turned in your National Insurance Card. See to it—there's a good chap.'

During the afternoon, Fielding read more of *Clarissa*. It was, he decided, a work of obsession; its detailed and unhurried logic, its long and loving repetitions, demonstrated its author's total commitment and belief. The reader too believed, believed so completely that he became at first fascinated and then disgusted by a world clogged with so much greed, complacency, prudishness and spite. Every time Fielding reached a temporary saturation point, he looked out of the window for ten minutes; but the Yugoslav landscape still rolled about as boringly as ever, and the only relief was an occasional crude farm building, some sullen cattle or a group of chunky children waving at a wayside halt. Four o'clock, five o'clock, six. Nothing had happened all day, and in half an hour he must go for his early dinner.

That evening at 5.30 plump Maisie had a visitor who was called Somerset Lloyd-James, MP. This gentleman had been a client of Maisie's for nearly eight years, with only a brief interval some three years back when there had been, through no real fault of either's, a minor misunderstanding. Now, after he had finished pretending to be a newly pubescent schoolboy whom Maisie, the under-matron, was seducing in the sick-room, Somerset Lloyd-James said:

'Fielding Gray. He *did* come to see you before he left?'

'Yes, Nugent.'

Nugent was the name which Somerset had chosen for the schoolboy.

'That's enough for that for now. What I want to know is, what did Fielding ... seem to feel about this trip to Cyprus?'

'Nothing in particular. Should he have done?'

'Lots of people would have been very pleased at an

assignment like that.'

'He wasn't. He was sorry if anything.'

'Ah,' said Somerset: 'why?'

'I don't think he likes the people much—after what they did to his face.'

'So that when he comes up with his stuff he'll do his worst for them?'

'He certainly won't kill himself finding excuses for them.'

'Thank you,' said Somerset Lloyd-James, MP: 'that's what I wanted to know ... You can call me Nugent again now. Matron, I've got such a frightful pain—just here. Do you think I could have a day in the sicker?'

Maisie suppressed a sigh.

'I'm sorry to hear that, Nugent mi.,' she said: 'you'd better lie down there and let me have a look at you ...'

Tessie Buttock was sitting fatly on the fender in the front hall of her hotel.

'Woozums, woozums,' she intoned to Albert Edward, who was lying in a rocking chair, 'how we do miss that ugly Fielding, to be sure. All those interesting chats about his writing friends and all their filthy habits. Not to mention what he pays so regular for his room. We're not so full these days, woozums darling, that we can forget about that.' She reached over and rocked Albert Edward's chair. 'It might even be a mercy if they decided to pull the old place down. They'd have to pay quite a bit for the compensation. But then Fielding would have nowhere to come home to.' A jagged smile cut into her mean, fleshy face. 'You see, woozums, this is the only home he's got. All he's got in the world is those dirty writing friends, and some trollop up west, and the pair of us. I wonder—don't you wonder, woozums?—what he's doing now.'

What Fielding was doing just then was walking down the corridor to the Yugoslav dining-car. Since this had been put on next to the wagon-lit coach for Athens, he had only a short way to go; and in fact it was even shorter than he expected, because the door at the end of the sleeping-car was locked.

Now he came to think of it, no one had come through to announce dinner; he had simply assumed that this would be at 6.30 as notified by the printed slip on his table at lunch, and he had therefore left his compartment promptly though unsummoned at 6.29. Perhaps there was some sort of delay (trouble with the cooking apparatus, trouble with the staff) and the door had been locked to fend off importunate diners till all was ready. Then surely the head waiter or one of his underlings would have been hovering with explanation or reassurance? But then again, he thought, this was an iron curtain country (more or less), and such places were notoriously careless of one's convenience. Perhaps the sleeping-car attendant would know what was going on.

The attendant had a cubby hole at the other end (the front end) of the sleeping-car. When Fielding reached it, its door was open and it was deserted. This in itself meant nothing. What was mildly worrying, however, was that the pile of passengers' passports, which were entrusted to the attendant and which Fielding had several times seen stacked on his table when going to and from the loo, had disappeared; and what was more discouraging still was that at this end of the car as at the other the connecting door was locked.

Calm, calm. Proceeding back along the carpeted corridor, Fielding knocked, one by one, on the doors of the compartments. One by one, as he received no answer, he opened them, only to find that in each case the compartment was empty; not only empty, but swept, garnished, pristine, unspotted by the least trace of occupancy past or present. When he opened his own door, which was half-way along, he stepped back, on sudden impulse, in case of ambush or trap; but it was exactly as he left it. Nor did this bring comfort, for a presence there, however alien, might have offered information, would certainly have offered human company, for which he suddenly yearned. The remaining doors, between his own and the end, he flung open, desperate and sweaty, without knocking. Nobody. Nothing. Once more he tried the door through to the dining-car: immovable as the gate of a tomb.

For some time now the train had been gradually slowing down. He looked out of the window. Dark now, nothing to see ... but surely ... lights, the lights on the rest of the train? But of course, unless the train was on a bend he wouldn't see them. One way to settle it. He forced down the window in the side door next to him and thrust his head into the night. Far away, in the direction from which the train had come, there was a single red light, receding: otherwise nothing, total blackness. And forward? Nothing at all, beyond the yellow-lit window at the front end of the sleeping-car, nothing at all except some kind of looming mass, darkness visible, as it were, which was near, how near?—nearer anyhow, suddenly all above him, *now* ...

The train (train?) must have been swallowed by a tunnel. Not four feet from him the light from the corridor window played on a furry black wall. The speed was still decreasing; but just as the wheels seemed about to stop entirely, they gathered way again, first slightly, then definitely, then vigorously. There must be a slope, he thought; there's nothing to pull it, nothing now except this lone car and me alone in it. Where? Why? How? Never mind that, only one thing to think about—escape.

Escape? From a runaway coach doing thirty miles an hour in a tunnel? Nothing for it. Wait. Perhaps it will slow down again, stop. Different noise from the wheels now, lighter, less confined, must be coming out. Slowly, surely. With God's grace it will stop. *God, make it stop.*

As the coach passed with a whoosh out of the tunnel, he put his head out of the window again. Far below he could see lights, as of a fair-sized town. The coach, so far from stopping, lurched violently round a bend. The thing was now quite clear. He was descending and rapidly accelerating round a series of loops, and at the next bend or the next but one the coach, unbraked, would simply ride off the rails into space.

Get out. Now. How? ... Jump *inwards*, towards the hill-side. But even so, rails, fences, wires, rocks, God knew what beside. Sleeping-car: *bedding.* He started back towards his compartment. The coach kicked and tilted, throwing him heavily against the side of the corridor; but after a grating of metal and creaking of wood the *status quo ante* was resumed. Last chance: out before the next corner. He flung into his compartment, seized the piled blankets from the upper bunk. The mattress, use it as a shield. Loaded with mattress and blankets, he staggered back along the corridor to the two side doors at its rear. He wrapped blankets round his loins and round his head; threw open the door which faced away from the gulf below; wrapped his arms and hands in two more blankets; clasped the mattress to his stomach, so that it shielded him from his face down to his lower shins; and then, as the wheels began to grind and squeal against the rails, he took off at a slant (head slightly forward) from the iron steps which descended from the open door. His last thought, as he fell into blackness, was of Gregory Stern's Mezuzah, which he was carrying, wrapped in a handkerchief, in the inner breast pocket next his heart: let the holy name of Shaddai save him if It would.

3: Intimations and intimacies

'I bought this stuff for you off the peg,' said Captain Detterling: 'I hope it fits.'

'It looks rather Greek,' Fielding said.

'It came from the best men's shop in Athens. Now you get dressed, while I settle up with these hospital people, and we'll be on our way.'

Detterling sauntered out of the room with a characteristic air of owning the entire building, and Fielding began to put on the clothes from the best men's shop in Athens. The shoes were hideous and the trousers disagreeably wide at the bottoms. Furthermore, while Detterling had bought him a grey homburg (of the type worn by old-fashioned Greek gentlemen when sitting outside cafés) which wasn't at all necessary, he had forgotten to get any underpants, which were. But who am I to complain? Fielding thought: I'm bloody lucky not to be wearing a shroud.

In fact, things could have hardly fallen out more fortunately. Less than an hour after the sleeping-car derailed itself a search-party from the town below had found Fielding, who was lying by the line suffering from multiple minor abrasions and immobilised by shock. Everyone had been extremely kind and helpful. He had been patched up by a competent doctor, made very comfortable in a private room in a local hospital, and treated with respect, the next morning, by an English-speaking policeman, who was distressed, however, that Fielding had no 'piece of identification'. At

Fielding's suggestion, a telephone call had been made to Captain Detterling at the Grande Bretagne in Athens, and two days later here Detterling was, bearing the new clothes which the kind-hearted policeman had warned him Fielding would need after his violent misadventure, and having apparently fixed everything to everyone's satisfaction.

There was a knock on the door, and Detterling re-entered with a puzzled look.

'They don't want any money,' he said crossly; 'they say that in communist countries medical care is free.'

'Are private rooms free too?'

'I mentioned that. They said that you were a guest who had suffered a grave misfortune in their country and was entitled to the best they could offer in recompense.'

'The Greek thing about hospitality, I suppose. This far south the people are Macedonians rather than Slavs.'

'I wouldn't know about that,' said Captain Detterling, 'but I find all this sweetness and charity very irritating. Personally, I like to pay the piper myself, so that I can call a disagreeable tune if I feel like it ... Do you approve of that homburg?'

'I'd sooner have had some pants.'

'It's bad form,' said Detterling, 'to go bare-headed in foreign countries—particularly poor ones. It looks as if you're saying, 'Why should I bother to dress properly in a mucky little place like this?' The poorer the country, the more correct one should be in one's *tenu*.'

'I don't doubt it. But I should still have liked some pants.'

'We'll get you a pair on the way through Thessalonika.'

'We're going by car?'

'Embassy car from Athens,' Detterling said: 'when one's dealing with these Bolshevik chappies it's as well to put on a bit of a show.'

As the car thumped along the pitted roads towards the border, Detterling explained how matters had been arranged. As a Member of Parliament, he had been well received at the Embassy in Athens, the First Secretary of which had luckily served during the war in his (and Fielding's) old regiment.

'Before your time, of course,' Detterling said, 'but when I vouched for you that clinched the matter. He made some telephone calls, including one to Belgrade, and turned over this jalopy complete with chauffeur, and by the time I got to the border on the way up there was a security big-noise waiting for me, waving your passport in the air and bursting to tell me the official story.'

'Which was?'

'On their version, the police had had a tip-off, now thought to be bogus, that a pair of escaped prisoners had boarded the train at Skopje. So they stopped it for a check-up at some little station farther down the line, and of course the sleeping-car attendant had to get down and account for his bodies, of whom by that time you were the only one left.'

'I remember stopping at several stations after Skopje, but I can't remember any kind of search.'

'Well, according to my man the attendant was called out to show them your passport, did just that, and then went off back to his post in the sleeping-car. What they didn't know till later was that he never got there. He was found in the cleaning cupboard of the station loo some hours afterwards with a large lump on his nut and still hanging on to your passport.'

'All right. But how did the coach ... break loose?'

'They're not too clear about that. But the theory is that with the attendant out of the way some wicked person or persons were able to unlink all the carriages behind you, and unlink you from everything in front, and then shove you off on a branch line and send you whizzing down the mountain-oh.'

'Pretty expert job.'

'That's what I thought. Mind you, it's the sort of thing guerillas and that lot were always doing during the war, and Yugoslavia was swarming with 'em. I dare say they kept in practice ... Anyhow, it seems that about a hundred yards from where you were found the coach took off, plunged down the mountain, fell over a cliff and was smashed to pieces on some rocks at the bottom. There's not a particle of your kit to be found, my man said, and there wouldn't have been a particle of you if you'd still been with it. For all of which, I am to convey to you a hundred thousand apologies from the President and People of Yugoslavia.'

'But do they know *why*?'

'Oh yes. The man told me with a poker face that it was probably an extremist group expressing their disapproval of the luxurious habits of capitalists and foreigners. A protest, you might say, against the International Company of Wagons-Lits.'

'You didn't let him fob you off with that?'

'I was eating his luncheon, old man. It would have been rather pointed—don't you think?—to contradict.'

'Darling,' said Isobel Stern in London, 'I *think* that at last this is it. Anyway, I'm late.'

'We shall have a fine son,' said Gregory.

'And I shall have a groaning,' she said.

About twenty-four hours after they left the hospital in Yugoslavia, Fielding and Captain Detterling drove past Mount Olympus. All of it, except the lower slopes, was hidden in thick, fierce cloud.

'The gods must be sulking,' said Detterling.

'I expect it's this.'

Fielding felt in his breast pocket and took out Gregory Stern's Mezuzah. He had found this, when he finally came to his senses in the hospital, tightly clasped in his right hand. Since it had been in the breast pocket of his coat when he jumped, and since the coat, ripped half to pieces, had been (he was told) some yards away from him when he was discovered, this was not easy to explain. Fielding imagined that he must have searched for and found the Mezuzah while still delirious. Such a notion was curiously affecting and much increased his regard, already considerable, for Stern's gift.

'What is it?'

'A sort of Jewish charm. Just the thing to upset Zeus and his crew. A present from Gregory. Which reminds me...'

Fielding went on to give Detterling the substance of Gregory Stern's messages. When he finished, Detterling said:

'He's wrong about the Cavafy memoirs. We must have them if we can. If he won't pay for them, I will.'

'He seemed very sure about it.'

'I hope,' said Detterling, 'that this new Jewish act of his is only on the surface. I've no objection to his giving you amulets or whatever, but if he lets it affect his judgment ... if he suddenly wants to be forever doing Jewish books by Jewish authors ... then it'll be very awkward.'

'There's no sign of that.'

'I've been working with him for three years now. I'm fond of him, and I know him really rather well; and I can tell you for certain that any time up to six months ago this Cavafy book would have been just the sort of thing to make him dribble at the mouth. The memoirs of a modern Greek poet who specialised in erotic themes with a strong historical flavour ... Quite irresistible. But now? Now he just dismisses it as one more "bugger book". And why? Because Cavafy is in the Hellenist tradition, whereas Gregory's getting obsessed with the Judaic. I'm going to put a stop to that rubbish if I have to beat it out of him.'

In the seventeen years, on and off, that Fielding had known Detterling he had never seen him so heated. That this blasé and elegant aristocrat should suddenly fly into a passion on behalf of a minor Greek lyric poet was a real eye-opener.

'I never knew you were so involved,' Fielding said.

'Neither did I,' said Detterling, his voice crackling with irritation, 'or not until a few weeks ago. I woke up one morning, after a late sitting of the House, with a terrible liver and one word hammering in my head: lies. I'd spent half the previous night, half the previous decade come to that, listening to politicians on both sides of the House mouthing out great big greasy *lies*. On the other hand, the one thing which had always impressed me, since I first joined in with Stern, was the extent to which those authors of his were concerned to tell the truth. They were a scabby lot, most of them, cranks and socialists and cheque-bouncers and niggers, but at least each of them, in his own dotty way, had a—how shall I put it?—a *hankering* for the truth. And suddenly that morning, while my liver festered and my head thumped, this seemed to be a remarkable and even a very moving thing. I became, as you put it, involved.'

'And yet,' said Fielding, 'a good half of us are professional liars. Novelists, certainly. We record what never occurred.'

'But unlike politicians you admit that before you start. Your truth has nothing to do with actual facts. Your truth consists in taking theoretical characters in theoretical situations and then tracing what you think would be the practical, moral and emotional consequences. If we, your readers, respond by saying "Yes, yes, that is how it would be", then you have told the truth.'

'Very often,' said Fielding, 'we just trick you into that response. Later on, when you close the book, you realise you've been conned ... that it's all been done with mirrors and not by real creative magic.'

'An interesting point,' said Detterling. 'But I suppose in that case we can just be grateful to you for a brilliant illusion. At least you're only using your trickery to entertain, not to impose your own will on other people's lives ... Which brings us away from my involvement and on to yours. How are *you* involved?'

'In general——'

'—Not in general,' said Detterling softly; 'here and now. You are, it seems, at present involved in such a project and in such a way that someone has just tried to ... do ... you ... in.'

'We can't be certain that what happened was deliberately aimed at me.'

'No. But we can be certain—or at least I can—that the Yugoslavs couldn't wait to get you out of their country. No request, you notice, that you should stay and help with the enquiries. Just, "So glad you've come, Mr Detterling, and please take him away as soon as he can move." They know there's someone after you, you see, and they don't want your corpse on their hands. Or so I should surmise.'

Fielding looked back at Mount Olympus. The clouds were less angry and were beginning to lift. Now that I'm receding, he thought, and taking the Mezuzah with me, the gods are starting to smile again. Perhaps the sacred name of Shaddai is not a blessing but, here at least, a curse.

'I was warned,' he said to Detterling abruptly. 'It's no good my pretending. I was warned, and so what happened must have been meant for me. What shall I do?'

'Take the first plane home from Athens.'

'No. Not now I've come this far.'

'Don't be obstinate, Fielding.'

'It's not that. It's what you were talking about just now— a hankering for the truth.' Fielding explained the genesis of his mission; how he had been reluctant at first, then half tempted by the chance to write revengefully of Cyprus, and finally won over by the personal nature of Tom's appeal. 'So you see,' he said, 'when I started I wasn't in the least concerned with the truth. Rather the reverse. But now ... now they've done this.... I must go on. To return now would mean that I'd allowed myself to be bullied—bullied out of my right to know.'

'Idiotic pride,' Detterling said.

'Partly. I don't like being denied. But there's also real curiosity. If someone has gone to such lengths, there must be something worth uncovering—don't you agree?'

'If someone has gone to such lengths, he'll go to greater.'

'I shall ask for protection.'

'If you ask for protection, you'll just be told to go home.'

'There must be a way.' His one eye pleaded. *'Res unius, res omnium,'* he said, quoting the motto of their old regiment.

'It's just conceivable,' said Detterling at last, 'that I know of someone who might help.'

In London, Somerset Lloyd-James, MP, called on the Most Honourable the Marquis Canteloupe.

Lord Canteloupe was a conservative peer who had been given minor office under the Government, some years before, as Parliamentary Secretary for the Development of British Recreational Resources, an appointment considered apposite since he had been long and profitably engaged in exploiting his own west country estate as a popular pleasure ground. Although his efficacy on the national scale was somewhat impaired by a feudal manner and a low habit of mind, he had shown undeniable talents in the field of publicity and advertisement. He had therefore been put in charge of a newly formed Department of Public Relations and Popular Media, on the strict understanding that he should confine himself to devising propaganda and take no overt part in its dissemination.

The noble lord's job was to ensure, as far as possible, that the views which the nation formed of events domestic and foreign were the views which suited the Government. This was very far from easy; the newspaper editors, the radio and television producers, through whom, for the most part, he must operate, were not at all inclined to adopt Lord Canteloupe's line simply on Lord Canteloupe's suggestion. However, he had found that a *quid pro quo* in the shape of some juicy giblet of 'inside information' would often win him a degree of co-operation, and he had become skilled in the confection of confidential items true enough to pass immediate scrutiny, false enough to give the impression he wanted to give, and apparently significant enough to earn editorial gratitude. In these semantic exercises he was assisted by a Member of Parliament called Carton Weir (who represented the Department in the Commons) and also, less officially but even more effectively, by Somerset Lloyd-James, who had long been editor of an influential journal called *Strix* and was happy to offer up his expertise in exchange for his lordship's patronage.

On this fine April morning their meeting had almost the appearance of an allegorical tableau: Somerset, with his scrawny limbs, bald head and pasty complexion, might have represented Winter in cringing withdrawal, while Canteloupe, with his vigorous and multi-hued presence, was for all his years the embodiment of sappy Spring. But any such interpretation of the scene would have been mistaken, for it was Somerset whose authority prevailed.

'Cyprus,' Somerset said: 'I don't like it.'

'Not *more* wog-trouble?'

'Only if it's deliberately stirred up. We've been at great pains to put over a reassuring image. In Cyprus, we have conveyed, reasonable concessions have been made in response to reasonable and democratic pressures. So all, we have implied, is now peace and contentment; there has been no retreat, only a diplomatic adjustment.'

' "Please adjust your dress before leaving",' Canteloupe interjected. 'Then you can pretend you never went in there.'

'We therefore ring down the curtain,' Somerset continued firmly, 'amid restrained but real applause, and forget the whole affair. So the last thing we want, the last thing your Department wants, is for the drama to be started up again —and there is no immediate reason why it should be. But if someone goes out there deliberately looking for trouble, trouble there will certainly be.'

'Well, it won't be our fault any more. Whatever happens there now, provided our troops stay in their bases and don't interfere, no one can blame us.'

'As to that, you may be right and you may not. But suppose someone goes raking up the past? Suppose,' said Somerset Lloyd-James, 'that someone starts upsetting the mild and convenient historical version which we have at last persuaded the country to accept? Suppose someone gets up on television and demonstrates—*demonstrates*, Canteloupe—that from the start of the Cyprus business to the finish Great Britain was bullied and blackmailed and betrayed, and in the sum was cheated out of millions of money, hundreds of soldiers' lives, and a good slice of her rapidly dwindling prestige?'

'They can't cut *my* head off,' Canteloupe said.

'You'd look very foolish. And your Department would have a lot of explaining to do.'

'But why should anyone ... demonstrate all that?'

'Because it happens to be demonstrable—if someone should find the right clues. Now then. Tom Llewyllyn, who has an instinct for this sort of thing, has sent Fielding Gray, who is no fool and knows the background, out there to investigate. If Fielding picks up the clues, he'll follow them through to the bitter end, and Tom, who has been promised a free hand by the BBC, will broadcast the result on television. So what do we do?'

'We have a drink,' said Canteloupe, and went to the cabinet by the wall.

'Not for me,' said Somerset; 'it's only ten-thirty.'

'One needs to be flexible in this game.'

Canteloupe poured himself a generous quintuple and followed it with a derisory squirt of soda.

'It is I,' said Somerset, 'who have been flexible so far. I got on to the Director of Features at the Television Centre and persuaded him to give an authoritative hint to Tom that a little delay would be appreciated.'

'How did you persuade him to do that?'

'I promised him, in your name, that you'd let him do a documentary film of your place in Wiltshire. Private rooms and Rembrandts included. Free.'

'Damn your beady eyes. I could have got thousands.'

'It'll be excellent publicity.'

'I don't need publicity. My place in Wiltshire,' said Canteloupe proudly, 'is at the top of the Stately Homes popularity poll.'

'You don't need the money either. You're richer than half the Dukes.'

'Half the Dukes are broke.'

'Anyway,' said Somerset patiently, 'it was worth it. The Director had a word with Tom, and Tom, under protest wired Fielding Gray in Athens and told him to hang on there for a possible change of instructions.'

'And what did Fielding Gray do?'

'They haven't yet heard from him.'

'Thousands of quid down the drain to get that telegram sent, and you don't even know he'll get it.'

'He'll get it. Copies have gone to every major hotel and also to the airport. So at the very latest he'll get it when he goes there to catch his plane to Cyprus.'

'All right,' said Canteloupe, impressed; 'but what then? All that anyone's agreed to is delay.' He sucked down his whisky and poured himself another without noticing. 'You say Tom Llewyllyn's been promised a free hand. When he thinks the delay's gone on long enough, he'll tell Gray to get going again, and what do we do then? *Give* the BBC my bloody house and ask for *more* delay? They'll probably want the park thrown in.'

'You know and I know,' said Somerset, 'that there are other people even more concerned than we are to stop Fielding writing this programme. By engineering this delay, we have given them time and opportunity to ... er ... make their point.'

'What a perfect swine you are,' said Canteloupe happily. 'But in that case, why not just leave it all to them? Why make the BBC send a million telegrams round the place, when all we need to do is *let* Gray go to Cyprus and get his come-uppance there?'

There was a knock on the door, through which floated a pudgy young man in a cloud of Chanel Eau de Cologne. Carton Weir.

'Get out,' said Canteloupe.

Carton Weir floated out again.

'I'd give that fat little pansy the push tomorrow,' said Canteloupe, 'but the PM insists on my keeping him. I can't think why.'

'He's particularly good at apologising to the people you insult. His *forte* is cleaning up messes. You may well need him—if there's a mess, for example, about Cyprus.'

'I'd far sooner have you.'

'I,' said Somerset, 'shall not be seen dead here if once there's a serious mess.'

'I might have known. Well, while you are here,' said Canteloupe, 'answer my last question. If there are all these people so anxious to settle the problem of Gray, why not leave them to it? Why do we have to get in on the act?'

'Because,' said Somerset, 'if anything happens to him in

55

Cyprus, it will be enquired why he was there and what he was doing, and this could lead to just the kind of revelations we deprecate. If, on the other hand, we delay him, thus giving other interested parties time to ... deflect him ... before he gets there, the connection with Cyprus will be far less pointed. And now I must get back to *Strix*. Please take my advice and be polite to Carton Weir.'

When Fielding and Captain Detterling reached the Grande Bretagne Hotel in Athens, there was a telegram waiting for Fielding:

DESIRABLE YOU WAIT IN ATHENS UNTIL FURTHER NOTIFIED AMUSE TOI BIEN TOM.

'Somebody else getting the wind up,' Detterling said. 'Be a good boy and go home.'

'He doesn't say that. He says I'm to wait here and amuse myself.'

'The more fool him. Athens is about as amusing as Wolverhampton.'

They went out into Constitution Square and took a taxi up to the Acropolis. For some reason this was closed, so they walked down-hill through the pine-trees and along a broad, noisy road to the entrance of the Agora. At the far end of this was a long portico of brash white stone. 'The American School's reconstruction of the Stoa,' said Detterling. 'Personally, I prefer ruins to stay ruined.'

'Let's try walking in it ... like philosophers of Athens.'

The April sun was hot enough to make the shade very grateful, and the marble pavement, they found, favoured a steady yet effortless walk, as of two officers pacing the yard of Buckingham Palace between the Old Guard and the New.

'I'm going to wire Tom,' said Fielding, 'and tell him I want to move on straight away.'

'Why not do as he says? He must have his reasons for asking.'

They turned about, both of them unconsciously using the standard parade-ground drill for the purpose, each in perfect time with the other, and marched slowly back along the portico.

'I suspect his reasons are too similar to yours in telling me to go home. I must move on quickly before they stop me altogether. If I get up enough momentum, they won't be able to. What was that?'

'What was what?'

'Something moved. Just behind us in that doorway.'

They checked and turned, again with military precision. The door to which Fielding now pointed was locked; just to one side of it was a statue of a boy with a flute, ears pricked, eyes leering along the pipes, legs crossed daintily half-way up the shin. Something about the full lips, as they curved over the flute, something about the firm but tenderly dented chin, made Fielding shiver all down his body.

'You're jumping at shadows,' Detterling said as they resumed their march.

'It was that boy's face. I . . . recognised it as we passed.'

'Of course you did. It's one of a thousand copies. Now then. If you're so set on going on with this business, I know a way you can get up momentum, as you put it, while obeying Llewyllyn's instructions at the same time. You remember I told you I knew someone who might help?'

'Yes.'

'Well, just now he's on the island of Hydra. Two hours from the Piraeus by boat. You can go there for the day, tomorrow if you like, and be back for dinner. I may as well come too. Introduce you and all that.'

'Who is it?'

'He's called Max de Freville.'

'The gambler?'

'Right. He used to run a very big chemmy game in London.'

'Then ran into trouble and came to live abroad with what he had left?'

'Which wasn't peanuts. Yes,' said Detterling, 'that's the chap. I think, though, he's now got some idea of starting a casino out here, if they'll let him. He's bored with doing nothing.'

'How can he help me?'

'He had a kind of hobby. He used to pay informants all over Europe to let him know what was going on behind the scenes. His own private intelligence service . . . very expensive. In the end, it became such an obsession that it nearly beggared him . . . only he had the sense to pack it all in and move out while there was still time.'

They turned about.

'Some three years ago,' Detterling went on, 'just before he

left London for good, Max had a kind of boasting fit and told me a lot of what he'd learnt over the years. He was being pretty wild that evening, but some of it was true all right, and some of it was in much the same area as this enquiry of yours. That could be true too.'

'Can you remember it?'

'Not in any detail. But I dare say Max can, and now he's had three years to calm down in, what he says should be worth listening to.'

'I don't suppose he could ... protect me?'

'He can tell you who to stay away from. He might even know of possible allies. I gather he still does a bit of nosing about ... as far as he can afford it.'

'And then,' mused Fielding, 'if he did give me a useful line, I could tell Tom I was really on to something and go right ahead—whether he liked it or not.'

'But would the BBC go on paying?'

'The BBC is very generous. They paid handsome expenses cash down and also an advance of fifty per cent on my full fee.'

'They might tell you to apply these resources in some other direction.'

'They might but I shan't. They got me into this and the least they can do is to let me see it through. Hydra to-morrow then?'

'Hydra tomorrow. I'll wire Max to expect us.'

They marched away across the Agora. The boy with the flute piped silently on as the lock turned in the door beside him and a face almost as still as his own looked out after the two retreating Englishmen.

'Darling,' said Isobel Stern to Gregory over their breakfast, 'I was right.'

'You're sure?'

'Either that, or I'm very, very late, which I never have been before.'

'Then our son will be born at Christmas.'

'Don't go getting ideas,' Isobel said.

Above the little harbour of Hydra the plain but handsome white houses, built by the pirate captains of old, rise by steep tiers into the hills. In one such house, about a quarter of a mile above the northern wing of the harbour, Max de

Freville put down his binoculars and said:

'They're just getting off the boat.'

'Let me look,' said Angela Tuck.

Angela was not Max's mistress but his comrade. For some years now they had spent much of their time together because they enjoyed taking care of each other. Although they often shared the same bed, they merely held hands in it, as innocent as the Babes in the Wood.

'I can recognise Detterling,' Angela said now, 'by the walk. As though he was wearing spurs. And there's a man with him dressed in the most ghastly suit and one of those homburgs. Are you sure that's Fielding Gray?'

'That's what the telegram said. I've never met him. How long since you did?'

'Seventeen years.'

'Well then, of course he's changed. And he's been badly disfigured, or so they tell me.'

'It's not that. He's got so fat, so coarse.'

'So have you,' said Max. 'Let's go down and meet them.'

They went through a little courtyard, out of a door and into an alleyway, along the alleyway and then down a flight of steps. At the bottom of the steps Detterling was consulting a surly islander, who was withholding information against the sight of money, while his companion in the homburg stood hunched against a wall. Max, pleased with this little piece of genre, screwed up the great furrows between his nostrils and the corners of his mouth in an expression which, intended for a smile, more nearly resembled the mask of tragedy.

'Welcome, old friend,' he boomed.

The islander slunk off, Detterling and his companion turned, saw Angela, removed their hats.

'Your hair,' cried Angela to Fielding; at least you've kept your hair.'

Fielding looked blankly at the large-limbed woman with the raddled, sexy face.

'It's been a long time,' said Angela, resigned to not being recognised but nevertheless sad. 'That summer in 1945. When me and Tuck had that house near yours in Broughton.'

Fielding shook his head, not in denial but in rejection. He knew this woman now; he remembered the summer of 1945 quite as clearly as she did; and most clearly of all he remembered that she had done him harm.

'I know, I know,' said Angela, reading his thought. She came down the steps and took his hand. 'We'll talk about *that* later,' she said. 'First of all, drinkies.'

Max and Detterling, who had been conferring together, started to loiter up the steps. Angela turned to follow them but Fielding took her arm and drew her back.

'It was all over long ago,' he said: 'no need to talk about it.'

'As you wish.' She put up her hand and quickly touched his hair. 'I was just sorry that you were brooding about it after all this time. I don't want it to spoil your visit.'

Fielding shrugged.

'We're taking the afternoon boat back to Athens,' he said, and led off after the couple in front. Detterling now introduced him formally to Max, who looked him over sharply for a second or two, and then remarked:

'Angela was very excited when she heard you were coming. You mustn't disappoint her.'

Before Fielding could think of a suitable reply, Max had turned back to Detterling.

'So I went to Rhodes first,' he said, 'but the authorities wouldn't hear of a casino there. Corfu, I knew, is just about to be fixed up anyway. So in the end I thought it might be worth taking a look round here.'

They all went through the courtyard, Angela several paces behind the three men.

'Surely,' Detterling was saying, 'if they do grant a concession here, they'll want a Greek to run it.'

'I know one who can front for me. An old chum called Lykiadopoulos. But somehow I don't think Hydra is right. Crowded in the summer, they say, but mostly with the arty set. All *they* bring to a casino is trouble.'

They trooped through a large living-room and out on to a terrace which looked south over the harbour. The steamer which had brought Fielding and Detterling was now beating busily away to the south-west for Spetsai and the Argolid. As he looked across the wrinkled sea to the coast of the mainland, Fielding saw that clouds were beginning to rise, somewhere, it must be, in the direction of Nauplion. A line of Virgil came into his head: *moriens dulces reminiscitur Argos;* dying, he remembers his sweet Argos. Leonard Percival walked on to the terrace.

'Morning, all,' he said. And to Fielding: 'Nice to see you again.'

Max introduced Percival to Detterling: Angela moved efficiently about with drinks and then went inside, muttering about the kitchen. Max and Detterling had already resumed their conversation about concessions, while Percival had seated himself in a canvas chair at the far end of the terrace and began to polish his glasses. Fielding came and stood accusingly over him.

'What are you doing here?' he said.

'I'm an old friend,' said Percival lightly. 'De Freville and I enjoy exchanging gossip, you might say. So being in this part of the world, and knowing he was too ... I'm delighted you've decided to join us. You've come to the right place.'

'What's that to you?'

'I am your sincere well-wisher,' said Percival, 'as you should have realised by now. I've already taken the liberty of telling Max about your assignment. You'll find him very helpful ... if you're polite.'

'I've come here as Detterling's friend and on his suggestion. I didn't need you to interfere.'

'My pleasure ... I was sorry to hear you had such an unpleasant time in Yugoslavia. All right now, I trust?'

'No thanks to you if I am.'

'Come, come. I warned you, didn't I?'

'You should have warned me properly, told me to get off the train. You knew what was going to happen?'

'In broad terms. Rather an imaginative scheme, we thought when we found out about it, and very apt. You see, *they* wanted you out of the way for good, and the longer no one knew it was you, the better. So *their* idea was,' said Percival with loving appreciation, 'to dispose of you in a remote district of a barbarous country, in such a way that you would be quite unrecognisable, and to make sure that your passport was nowhere around to identify you.'

'They don't seem to have been too clever about that. My passport was found soon enough.'

'Enthusiastic amateurs, that's *their* trouble. No attention to detail.'

'Who are "they"? Cypriots, I suppose. And who are *you* for that matter?'

' "They",' said Percival, 'are people who resent you sticking your nose in where it isn't wanted. *We*, on the other hand, are anxious that it should not be cut off, as we are hoping you will sniff out delicious truffles.'

'Then why did you bloody near let me get killed?'

'We wanted to make sure you were the right kind of man for our purpose. We had to know two things. One: were you a chap that would get cold feet at the first hint of danger? That was why I gave you a tip-off, told you to stay out of trouble and stick to your novels and so on—to see how you'd react. And true to your Dragoon upbringing, you didn't seize your luggage and run, you sat there on your arsehole and scowled. Good for you, chum, At the same time, you *were* cautious enough (quite rightly) to ask what could best be done, and this brings us to the second thing we had to find out. Granted you weren't the kind to scuttle away in a panic, were you competent to take care of yourself? Because if not, you were no use to us. So I was instructed to give you enough information to put you on the alert but not enough to let you know what was coming. All that palaver about restaurant-cars was to make sure you were awake and mobile about the time the trouble started. We owed you that, but the rest was up to you.'

'And have I passed your test?'

'You're still here, aren't you?'

'And if I'd failed?'

'It would have been indisputably clear,' said Percival, 'for the most cogent of all possible reasons, that you were quite unable to help us.'

'You bastard,' said Fielding.

He reached down, whipped Percival's spectacles from his face, and drew his fist back to strike. Percival blinked up at him.

'Please return my glasses,' he said: 'I can't see anything without them.'

The blinking, defenceless eyes were too much for Fielding.

'Here,' he said, and handed the spectacles tenderly back.

'You should understand,' said Percival equably, 'that *we* are a perfectly respectable organisation, British and proud of it, with high-level sanctions for all we do. In assisting us you will have nothing to be ashamed of.'

'What makes you think I'm going to assist you?'

'You already are. Because in any case at all your mission and your enquiry are exactly what we would wish them to be. Our only suggestion is, now that you've established your qualification in this line, that we should give you the benefit of our own expertise ... in return, of course, for regular reports on your progress.'

'And if I refuse?'

'Why should you? You'll be going ahead anyway, so why refuse the valuable support ... the valuable clues ... which we can offer. You see how highly we think of you.'

Fielding looked south over the harbour. The steamer had disappeared, had probably rounded the cape into the Gulf of Nauplion, from which, he now noticed, the clouds were rising much higher and darker than before.

'Dirty weather on the way,' said Percival, following his gaze. 'Look, old man. We know, in outline, all there is to know about the Cyprus affair from way back. What we want is for someone to follow it all up and then construct a detailed and water-tight account. That someone is you. We can set you up with all the main headings, so to speak, and tell you exactly where to go to check everything up and fill in the gaps. We'll give you the whole thing on a plate.'

'Then why not do it yourselves?'

'Because we, for obvious reasons, can't have anything to do with television. Not directly, at any rate. That's where you come in. Having got up your case, all the quicker and the surer for our discreet and unacknowledged assistance, you then present the incontrovertible facts to a shocked world. Believe me, you'll make quite a sensation.'

'Which for some obscene reason will also suit you?'

'Yes, but why should you worry? You may even be glad when you know more about it.'

Angela came round with more drinks.

'Lunch in five minutes,' she said. And then, looking away to the south, 'There's going to be a storm.' She shivered slightly, pursed her lips at Fielding, and went over to Detterling and de Freville. Everyone had been very careful, Fielding now thought, to leave Percival and himself undisturbed.

'You do realise,' he said, 'that even if I agree to do what you want, my employers in the BBC are having second thoughts?'

'Yes,' said Percival. 'There are those in high places who want to let sleeping dogs lie.'

'Why don't you then? You claim to be an official organisation ... British and proud of it.'

'Official interests can differ.'

'Evidently. So what happens if those in high places pre-
vail with the BBC and the whole thing's called off?'

'If you tell your friend Tom Llewyllyn what Max and I
are going to tell you,' said Percival, 'nothing—but nothing
—will make him agree to let it be called off.'

At lunch it was agreed that in view of the nasty weather
which was blowing up Fielding and Detterling would do
better to delay their return to Athens until the following
day.

'If it's rough,' Max said, 'the boat can't come into the
harbour because of the narrow entrance. It anchors outside
the bar and they row you out to it.'

'Rather alarming? In a rough sea.'

'They're very clever at it. But if it's really rough,' said
Angela, 'the steamer doesn't stop at all.'

Even as she was speaking a grey cloud moved over the
face of the sky and the wind gathered strength through the
alleyways.

'Goody,' Angela shivered.

'That settles it,' said Max. 'I can lend you both pyjamas.'

'And we shall have more leisure,' said Percival, 'to advise
our friend Major Gray.'

'Advise him about what?' Angela asked.

Angela did not take much interest in Max's intrigues, but
she was rather interested, now that he had risen out of her
past, in Fielding Gray. She had her own plans for his entertainment and was therefore anxious to know about other
people's in order to avoid unnecessary conflict.

'A little piece of journalism he's undertaken,' said Percival. 'Max and I may be able to help. This afternoon?' he
suggested.

Angela glanced quickly at Max, signalling, as clearly as
though she had spelt it out, what she had in mind. Max
took the point and shrugged good-humouredly.

'Not this afternoon,' he said to Percival, 'tonight. As you
say, we've plenty of time. After lunch, I for one am going
to have a siesta.'

Angela smiled at him gratefully.

'Snug,' she said. 'Nothing snugger than listening to the
storm outside and having a siesta.'

'Max mind?' said Angela. 'Of course not.'

She passed a hand along Fielding's flank and up towards his chest, keeping the palm flat as it passed over his hips and his belly.

'Max knows what I'm like,' she explained, 'and he'd much sooner it was you than one of the local fishermen. Although he's a very civilised man, he's also rather a snob.'

After lunch Max had disappeared. Angela had firmly offered Detterling and Percival a choice between backgammon and siesta, of which they had elected the former. She had then led Fielding off, allegedly to show him the room which he would share for the night with Detterling, and taken him, instead, to her own.

'Max generally sleeps here at night,' she said, 'but he uses his own room in the afternoon.'

After which, she had removed her skirt without ceremony and lain down on the bed in her stockings.

'Come on,' she said: 'show a bit of courtesy to your hostess.'

So now Fielding was showing her all the courtesy he could muster, though not without misgiving. Every now and again he would think of his host and his social skill would flag. Then Angela would reassure him and set him going again.

'Turn over,' she said.

As the rain rattled against the windows and Angela's fingers ran up and down his spine, Fielding thought of that far off summer during which Angela and her husband (now dead, it seemed) had occupied a house near his parents' on the coast at Broughton Staithe. He had desired her then, and she had first teased and later rejected him, and finally she had betrayed him. She had learnt his secrets and deliberately passed them to his enemies. So that now, now that it was himself, apparently, who was desired, he had the chance of revenge. The chance, he thought, but not the inclination; he was quite happy to lie there while this knowledgeable and still rather attractive woman kneaded his buttocks and his back. Yet why, he asked himself, *was* he desired? True, Angela could no longer afford to be so choosy as she had been at Broughton, but she could at least have found somebody whose face was still intact.

'Why now?' he muttered along the pillow. 'Why not *then*, when I was young ... unspoilt?'

Angela, who was crouching over him with her stockinged knees on either side of his own, lent forward to talk into his ear.

'You're still young,' she said, 'and I like you spoilt. *Then* you were perfect, I admit. But I could never fancy perfection. I've always preferred something that was slightly odd . . . even unwholesome.'

She eased her thumbs up the insides of his shoulder blades.

'That's why I seduced your friend Lloyd-James. Remember?'

Fielding remembered very clearly. Somerset Lloyd-James, his school friend and contemporary, had come to stay at Broughton that summer, and Angela had invited them both to her house while her husband was away in London. There and then, she had as good as undressed Somerset under Fielding's eyes and had only paused to order Fielding out of the house before making Somerset free of her. To this hour Fielding could still see them as they had been when he left the house, Angela's great honey thighs and Somerset's scraggy white ones.

'But of course,' Angela was saying now, 'if I'd known that evening all that I found out later, it's you I'd have gone for because it was really you that was unwholesome. Somerset was just rather misshapen physically. But you'—she ran both thumbs down to the top of the cleft between his buttocks—'you were tainted all the way through. What about that wretched boy at your school who killed himself—what was he called?——'

'—Christopher,' said Fielding, shivering with his distress at the memory and with the pleasure that came from her busy thumbs, 'Christopher Roland.'

'Christopher Roland . . . What about *him*?' she said.

'I loved him, that was all.'

'You loved him and he killed himself. What did you do to him, Fielding?'

'Must we talk about him?'

Somerset Lloyd-James had found out about Christopher and told Angela. Angela had betrayed Fielding to his mother. His mother——

'—Must we talk about Christopher?' he said. 'It caused enough unhappiness at the time.'

'Yes, we must,' she said. 'It excites me to talk about him.

Turn over, Fielding ... It excites you too, doesn't it?'

As indeed it did. For all the misery, the guilt, the despair which Fielding had once felt about the boy, for all the sadness which he still felt and the almost unbearable recollections of his mother's part in the affair, talking about Christopher had excited him beyond anything which Angela's ministrations could have achieved, skilful as they were.

'Show me, Fielding. Show me what you did with Christopher.'

'I ... Nothing. I wanted to be very gentle. So I put my arms round him, and I kissed him, and then he ... trembled ... and it was all over.'

Angela chuckled and ran her finger-nails along his arm.

'Poor little Christopher. And the next time?'

'There wasn't a next time. Christopher wanted there to be, but at first I didn't, because he was ... changed somehow, and anyway I was afraid we might be found out. There'd been talk already ... Go on, Angela, don't stop.'

'All right, if you go on about Christopher.'

'Well ... later on, when I thought it was safe ... I wanted to do it again. But it was too late, because Christopher ... because...'

'Because Christopher was dead.'

'*Don't stop.*'

'Fielding. Show me what you would have done. What you would have done to Christopher if he hadn't been dead.'

Later on, Angela said:

'What did he look like, the boy you wanted to do that to?'

'I don't really know how to put it. He was ... so finely made, so strong ... and yet so soft. I can't think of anyone like him. But yes,' said Fielding, 'yes, I can. Yesterday in Athens I saw a statue ... in that portico the Americans have built ... a statue of a boy playing the flute. The same legs, firm yet tender. The same lips, the same chin, the same face.'

'Now,' said Angela, 'I'm going to be Christopher. I'm going to imagine what he'd have done to *you* ...'

At dinner they all reassembled, some having had a more interesting afternoon than others. Although the wind was still screaming down the alleyways, the rain had stopped, and Max proposed that Fielding should accompany Percival and himself to the tavern down by the harbour.

'Angie would only be bored by the discussion,' Max said, 'and you can tell Detterling about it later if you want to. He can stay here and keep Angie happy.'

'Backgammon?' said Detterling to Angela.

'We'll see when they've gone,' she said.

For the second time that day she looked gratefully at Max.

Max, Percival and Fielding sat at a table by the window of the Taverna Poseidon. Pressure lamps hissed and a group of sailors, in a far corner, muttered about the price of fish. Outside, the wind swept the empty quay under the dim electric light, while the waters of the harbour slapped heavily at the rows of moored caiques.

'If it's only half as strong as this tomorrow,' Max said, 'they'll never get the steamer inside the bar of the harbour.'

Spiros, the tavern-keeper, brought them a large can of wine, three tumblers and a plate of wizened apples.

'What do you say, Spiros? Will the wind keep up?'

Spiros turned down the corners of his mouth and moved away. The sailors, observing this, nodded to each other in approval: one did not give valuable information to strangers just for the asking.

'Disagreeable fellow, that,' said Max: 'they all are here. They don't mind tourists in the summer, if only because they can cheat 'em rotten, but they hate it if you stay for any length of time. They think you're prying into their secrets.'

'Have they got any?'

'None. But their ancestors were pirates and they've inherited the pirate mentality. They regard this island as their lair and they don't care for people hanging about on it.'

'Least of all rival pirates,' said Percival; 'one does see their point. But they ought to be grateful to you. If you start up a casino here, it'll bring 'em more tourists to cheat rotten.'

'I've as good as decided against the place and they know it. I'll be moving on very soon.'

'Where next?'

'It occurred to me that the Cypriots might be interested.

I'm told they want to build up their tourist trade.'

'What a lot of time we all spend,' said Percival, 'thinking about that wretched little island.'

'Mind you,' said Max. 'I'd still need a Greek to front for me. I wouldn't trust the Cypriot Government to deal square with an Englishman. Not yet. Perhaps never ... after what's happened. Which brings us,' he said to Fielding, 'to the information which Leonard here says you're after. Shall I tell you why I don't trust the new Government in Cyprus?'

'Because the Cypriots dislike us,' Fielding said.

'But that's just the point. They don't dislike us. They never have. Which makes it all so much more sinister. If they'd just hated us, anyone could have understood their behaviour. But since, on the contrary, a lot of them even *loved* us, you'll agree that something very peculiar must have happened to set 'em off.'

'Enosis,' said Fielding; 'all that hysteria about self-determination. Surely you don't need to look any further.'

'You're taking the superficial view,' Max said. 'Of course they were ready to do a bit of shouting about Enosis and the rest of it, but they certainly didn't intend to have any real unpleasantness, any more than they did in the thirties. They just wanted a little excitement to liven up public holidays.'

'At first, possibly. But once they knew they had official support in Athens—which they *hadn't had* in the thirties— they began to take it seriously.'

'Superficial again,' said Max. 'British rule had its faults, but at least it was solvent and it was secure. It meant honest government, however short-sighted. Why reject this in favour of absorption by a corrupt and semi-bankrupt Balkan state, which would have taxed Cyprus into the sea and taken half its young men as conscripts?'

'The ethnic tie,' said Fielding. 'Besides, the Cypriots wanted to think they were choosing for themselves. They may have liked us but they hadn't chosen us. Here was their chance to assert themselves—with full encouragement in Athens from their own kith and kin.'

'There was encouragement all right,' said Max; 'but the most important part of it did not come from their Athenian kith and kin.'

'Oh come, come, come. I know the mainland Greeks don't care for their Cypriot cousins as much as they sometimes pretend to, but they were quite happy to lend a help-ing hand. If only to annoy the Turks.'

'Happy to break a few windows and shout a few slogans, yes. Not to spend good money.'

'Then where did the money come from?'

'Where does money always come from these days?' Leonard Percival said.

There was a long silence. Spiros came to their table, took away their wine-can although it was by no means empty, and returned with a full one. The sailors grinned at one another. Spiros had cheated the strangers of a good six drachmae.

'You're not going to tell me,' said Fielding at last, 'that the Americans——'

'—Look,' said Max. 'In the old days, as Detterling has told you, I used to spend the greater part of my money keeping myself informed. It started as a small service to check up on the people who came to my chemmy game—whether their credit was good; but one thing led to another and in the end I had correspondents all over Europe. Good ones too. Leonard here, for example, was one of them for years ... supplementing his meagre official income.

'Now, although I had to give up this amusing hobby some time ago, in the middle fifties my network was at its best, and one of the things I found out was this. The Americans, though they find us useful and don't really resent the little influence we still exercise, cannot and will not tolerate any survival of the imperial image. They cannot and will not suffer our retention of foreign *possessions*. This is not so much a matter of policy on their part as of sentiment: as long as any British colonies exist, they cannot forget that America was once a colony itself. Only by wiping out our entire colonial empire can they wipe out the indignity of their own colonial past. There are other considerations—it is much easier, for instance, to get American goods and industries into a place once you've got the British admini-stration out of it—but paramount is the determination, as you might say, to trample on the redcoats.'

'Neurotic envy,' Fielding said.

'Very probably. What made them so furious about Suez, for example, was not what we were doing but the fact that we were the people doing it, in our old territories and in the good old way. With kettle drums and drawn sabres, which by this time, on the American reckoning, should have been safely rusting in museums. Anyway,' Max continued, 'the anti-colonial sentiment, whatever its psychological origin, is so strong that the United States, from time to time, have gone as far as actually to encourage and finance the subversion of our colonies. Secretly, of course, so secretly that on an official level no one even has to dream about it. But none the less Uncle Sam's helping hand has often been decisive ... in Kenya for one place ... and in Cyprus for one more.'

'But *how*?'

'Flattery, advice and training for the local leadership; weapons and equipment; money. All provided on the q.t. by American secret agents. This was what they offered the Cypriots ... partly direct and partly through Athens; and the Cypriots, for very shame, had to pick up the weapons and fight. Poor Cypriots. One day they were happily yelling about freedom in the market-place ... and the next they found that someone had actually taken them at their word and given them brand-new rifles instead of empty ouzo bottles. It was now a matter of face: there could be no turning back.'

'All this is rather nebulous,' Fielding said. 'Say what you like about the American secret service, on the face of it the Cypriot rebels were commanded by the patriot, Colonel Grivas, and armed with smuggled weapons.'

'But who paid for the weapons? The Cypriots couldn't and the Greeks wouldn't. And as for the patriot Colonel Grivas,' said Percival, 'he was closely assisted at every step by a guerilla expert called Diomedes.'

'And so?'

'And so Diomedes was the *nom de guerre* of an American secret serviceman called Earle Restarick.'

'Restarick,' repeated Fielding: 'I seem to have heard the name.'

'Perhaps. He was mixed up with me in that business in Germany ten years ago.'

'That,' said Fielding with distaste.

'That,' said Percival. 'A project, you may remember, which Britain and the US had in common, so at that time we were on the same side. I found him a very interesting man.'

'And now you're claiming that this Restarick later became the brains behind Colonel Grivas?'

'The brains, and the bombs, and the cash.'

'How can you be sure?'

Percival dipped a slice of apple in his wine and bit it in two with a snap.

'In this game,' he said, 'you get to know a man's style. I was working in Cyprus during the trouble, and more and more of the tricks pulled by the other side had what one might call Restarick's *idiom* ... which I remembered very well from the job we'd worked on together in Germany. And then, later on, I received information which proved that he was in Cyprus at the time. For that matter, he's still there now.'

'Tell him about this idiom, this style,' said Max.

'Restarick's favourite trick was a kind of four-dimensional feint. He would persuade his opponent to believe—to believe absolutely—in some situation, tactical, moral or intellectual, which simply didn't exist. In his response to the pressures of this mythical situation, Restarick's opponent would eventually take the action or strike the attitude which Restarick required of him, without Restarick's having to move a finger himself. In the end, this opponent would probably aim a desperate blow at some illusory figure of Restarick's creation—and the blow would go right through the shadow and land where Restarick wanted it to land. Several times in Cyprus he manoeuvred British patrols into firing on one another or on innocent crowds, he tricked British agents into denouncing one another, he even blackmailed an important officer into putting a time-bomb under the Governor's bed. Beautiful work,' said Percival, 'pure Restarick. He's quite indifferent, by the way, to the human or political results. He's only concerned with the immediate problem proposed to him and finding the neatest solution.'

'Nevertheless,' said Fielding, 'although these exploits had Restarick's style, and although he was in Cyprus at the time, you can't *prove* that he was Diomedes.'

'No,' said Max; 'not yet. But we can if we have just one more link.'

'One more link,' said Percival. 'Pick up that link, achieve certain proof that Restarick was master-minding Grivas— and you can loose off the biggest anti-American scandal of a lifetime on twenty million television sets.'

'And where is this ... link ... to be found?'

'Concealed on a dead body,' said Max de Freville, 'in a tomb eight centuries old. It sounds rather bizarre, I agree, but the explanation is really quite logical...'

By the next day the wind had weakened, but not enough to allow the steamer from Athens to attempt the narrow entrance to the harbour. Two rowing boats were to convey passengers—at a cost of two drachmae per head for Hydriots, ten for other Greeks, and fifty for Fielding and Detterling—out to where the packet would anchor.

While Fielding and Detterling waited to embark, Max gave Detterling messages for friends in London (whither Detterling must shortly return), Angela drank several large ouzos in the Taverna Poseidon out of sadness at her guests' departure, and Percival ran over the instructions which Fielding had been given the previous evening.

'Remember,' said Percival, 'that *they* don't know either that this object exists or where it is hidden. So they won't be guarding it.'

'But they will be watching me.'

'Certainly. But if you just pretend to poke about, as though you haven't any particular line to follow, and then give 'em the slip, they won't know where you've gone or what you're up to.'

'Easier said than done. Besides, suppose they try some really radical expedient—as in Yugoslavia?'

'Unlikely. Restarick won't want to draw attention to Cyprus by murdering a well-known writer—who's there on behalf of the BBC—bang on the doorstep. Fielding Gray dead in Yugoslavia would have been well enough, but in Nicosia ... no. Odd as it may seem, the nearer you are to the centre of it all, the safer you'll be. From bodily harm at any rate.'

'What other sort do you have in mind?'

'Restarick,' said Percival, 'is devious. He has his plans festering away for the future, so he doesn't want a lot of inquisitive flies arriving in Cyprus to buzz round your corpse—because while they were at it they might sniff out even nastier lumps of putrescence. This means he wants you alive—at any rate as long as you're in Cyprus—but he also, for obvious reasons, wants you silent. So what does he do?'

'You tell me. You're the expert on Restarick.'

'He has recourse,' said Percival, 'to his favourite method. He brings pressure to bear on you by placing you in an exigent situation. Either a real one or, just as likely, an imaginary one which he's conjured up especially for you. In either case the pressure will be such—believe me, I've seen him at it—that you will be mentally anaesthetised, quite incapable of speaking a word in your own voice. That's the kind of thing you've got to watch out for with Restarick.'

The steamer came into sight round a headland and sounded its hooter. Bare-footed boys ran round in circles with luggage. Angela came red-eyed out of the Taverna Poseidon.

'So,' said Percival, 'the best of luck. You're absolutely sure where to find it?'

'Yes.' Fielding shuddered. 'You've made it very plain.'

Angela swayed up to them.

'I do wish you weren't going so soon,' she croaked.

'So do I,' said Fielding, thinking of her gartered stockings.

The oarsmen called from the rowing-boats. Percival started to hum the Regimental March of Lord Hamilton's Light Dragoons, and Detterling clanked along the quay in time to it. Max took Angela's hand and gave his grisly smile at her, while Fielding settled his deplorable homburg as tightly on his head as he could.

'That's right, old man,' said Percival: 'hang on to your hat.'

Into a rowing-boat among a muddle of baskets, carpet bags, caged chickens. Detterling breathing heavily beside him: both facing to stern. Angela waving and slobbering, Max saluting to the peak of his yachting cap, Leonard Percival slowly parting his teeth in a grin like a portcullis. Past a row of moored caiques, past a group of idle sailors hawking and jabbering on a jetty, and so we say farewell to dirty and dishonest little Hydra, and ... through the harbour bar.

At once it seemed as if the boat were standing on its stern and that chickens, carpet-bags, Fielding and all were being sucked straight into the sea. But just as he felt himself finally going the boat righted itself, dipped its bows, flung Detterling and himself back on to two squatting grandmothers in black. No one else had turned a hair: it was routine. Fielding and Detterling apologised, picked themselves up, barked their shins on the cross-bench, received a mass of flying spray on their trousers, and were sworn at by the boatman, who looked like Charon but rather more malignant. Huddled together on the floor, they achieved some kind of stability for the next three minutes, at the end of which, hearing greetings from above, they looked up to see the cold, black side of the steamer. About seven feet above them was a square opening, ten feet by ten, from which two rope ladders were now let down to their rowing-boat.

First up, agile as spiders, were the two grandmothers. Then a deck-hand came half-way down the right-hand ladder and gestured to Charon. The latter passed up a suitcase, which the deck-hand caught with a swing of his arm and released again a split second later, so that it flew out of his hand and up through the opening in the ship's side. This procedure was repeated until all baggage was disposed of, whereupon Charon signed to Fielding to make the ascent up the left-hand ladder, the right-hand one still being occupied by the deck-hand, who was apparently telling Charon some kind of anecdote. Since the rowing-boat was lying in the lee of the steamer and was therefore rocking very little, Fielding anticipated no trouble in getting himself on to the rope ladder. This he gripped, then ran his hands up it while he manoeuvred both feet on to the rowing-boat's gunnel. It was at this stage that Charon pushed his craft clear of the steamer with a brisk lever movement of one oar, at the same time tossing up a large and rusty matchet to the deck-hand on the second ladder, who, using the same powerful swinging arm action as before but opening his fingers a split second earlier, launched the tool edge foremost straight at Fielding's head.

4: The Castle

Tom Llewyllyn went to see Gregory Stern in his London office. After congratulating Gregory on Isobel's pregnancy and hearing the gratifying details of an American paperback deal in respect of his most recent book (*Queen Elizabeth II, The Bourgeois Monarch*), Tom said:

'I'm worried about Fielding Gray.'

'I'm the one to worry,' Gregory said. 'First the BBC steal you, my best modern historian, to run their idiot programme, and then you steal my best novelist and send him off like bloody Byron.'

'It wasn't *quite* like that, Gregory. And Fielding did need a change.'

'So he's having his change and now you tell me you're worried.' Gregory ran two fingers along his upper teeth and then prodded an incipient pimple on his jaw-bone. 'So what's he done? Burnt down the Parthenon?'

'He rang me up yesterday,' Tom said, 'yesterday morning. I'd sent him a telegram asking him to hang on in Athens for a bit in case we wanted to revise his instructions. And now here he is ringing up to say that he was going straight on to Cyprus, that I needn't think I could stop him, and that anyway it wasn't safe for him to stay in Athens.'

'Mad,' said Stern, waving both hands in the air; 'you've paid him so much money that you've made him mad. Cyprus ... He probably thinks he's Othello. Next time he rings up he'll be Tamberlaine going to Persepolis or Jesus Christ going up to his heavenly father. Why couldn't you leave him as he was—quietly writing novels in Buttock's Hotel?'

'Stop exaggerating, Gregory. Fielding certainly sounded rather light-hearted but he was perfectly lucid.'

'Lucid, you call it? All that about "not being safe for him to stay in Athens". What sort of talk is that?'

'There's still no need to exaggerate. I was hoping you might be able to suggest some sort of explanation.'

'How should I explain such *sotiserie*?'

'Well, I wondered,' said Tom, embarrassed and reluctant, 'whether Isobel had been having any more of those ... hunches ... of hers?'

'Isobel has no time for such rubbish. She is too busy bearing my son.'

'Of course ... Gregory, you've known Fielding for as long as I have. You know as well as I do that such behaviour is quite untypical. Will you please try to say something helpful.'

'What can I say, my dear?' said Gregory more soberly than he had spoken yet. 'Except that I always thought he wasn't so well balanced as he liked to appear.'

'What would you *do* if you were me?'

'In a very few days now,' said Gregory, 'Detterling will arrive back from Athens. Having spent hundreds of pounds of my money in the Grande Bretagne Hotel, he must at last condescend to come home and report. He will have seen Fielding, and he will tell us all about him. Detterling is an ex-officer and he will know what to do.'

'So are you an ex-officer. And so is Fielding, come to that.'

Gregory rose and went to the open window, through which came April bird-song and the evening trill of typists released to their lovers.

'With Fielding and me,' Gregory said, 'it was only ever skin-deep. Although we may have looked the part, we always really relied on somebody else—usually the loyal and capable sergeant-major. But Detterling is the genuine article. He decides everything for himself and he relies on no one but himself to carry his decisions through.'

'Then why did he end up as only a Captain?' Tom asked. 'He had a regular commission and nearly six years of war to prove himself. Younger men than him were made Generals.'

'I've often wondered about that,' said Gregory. 'one day ... not yet awhile, but one day ... I shall ask him.'

Fielding Gray walked up the path towards the Castle of Buffavento. At the bottom of the path, a hundred yards below him, the road up the mountain had ended in a small area of sand and stone, on which his taxi was now parked with its somnolent driver inside it. Below this again the mountainside, rock and scrub and fir, fell away for hundreds of feet and then checked its descent to undulate gently into the plain of the Mesaoria, whose livid blues and lush purples and treacly yellows made a huge cloth of motley on which the distant minarets of Nicosia were set like a tiny silver cruet.

Above him, as he walked slowly but steadily up the winding path, Fielding could see the Castle: low and scaly, like a dragon crouching along the ridge, legs splayed to clasp it. The sun was burning down from the zenith; there was no wind; the cicadas hummed morosely. The knights castellan, Fielding thought, did they walk up this path, at noon-day, in full armour? And what kind of armour did they wear, those old crusaders? Chain mail, plate armour, leather jerkins? Plate armour was surely very rare when this castle was first built, and by no means every knight could afford a coat of chain; but leather? Leather, he knew, could keep out steel, for did he not owe his own life to the leather band inside his homburg, which had been proof against the flying matchet? Yet somehow leather seemed beneath the dignity of a crusading knight, even if he were so poor and unimportant that he was condemned to make up one of the band that garrisoned this castle, a younger son and landless man, far from home and far from Jerusalem.

However that might be, even this suit (from the best men's shop in Athens) was uncomfortably hot. He stopped, set down the small grip which held his picnic lunch, lifted his homburg and wiped his forehead. Never mind; only another sixty or seventy yards to the top. Before starting again, he looked down at his taxi. How could the driver bear to stay inside that metal carapace (like plate armour) in this heat? And for that matter, the man ought to be up here with him if he was serious about his job. For the driver, Fielding knew, must be the man whom 'they' had told off to watch him. Whenever he asked the concierge at his hotel to send for a taxi, even for very short journeys inside Nicosia, the same man turned up in the same car. There could only be one explanation. Fielding did not resent his custodian and made no attempt to avoid him: better know by whom he was watched and how than tremble every time he passed a beggar. Besides, as he was demonstrating so clearly just now, the man was grossly inefficient—an amateur and not even enthusiastic. Lulled by several days' routine sightseeing in Fielding's company—Bellapaix, Salamis, Paphos —he had doubtless decided that Fielding had nothing to go on and was simply killing time. At first he had lurked behind Fielding round temples and theatres and museums, but by now he seemed thoroughly bored. Too bored, thought Fielding, to climb the steps to the Castle of Buffavento; for what (he imagined the driver as thinking) could this mouldering relic of the crusaders have to do with an up-to-date intrigue in a world of time-bombs and taxis? Sleep on, dull child of your age, soothed by the cicada.

Fielding replaced his hat, picked up his bag, and went on up the path. After a little, this brought him to a flight of straight and narrow steps, and these in turn to a small natural platform. To his right, a path led away to the east, along the very spine of the mountain ridge, between trees which grew just below it on either side. To his left a rather wider path ran some sixty yards to the castle gate, beyond which an open court was visible. Ignoring the castle for the moment, Fielding walked straight across the little plateau. Far below him, the glittering sea stretched north to the coast of Turkey, which seemed, in the distant haze, like some long white flickering wave slowly rolling towards him.

He shook his head to dispel this illusion and walked along the path to the castle. Pausing in the courtyard, he could have sworn that he heard the splash of water. Why not? There must be a spring up here somewhere, or the castle would have been indefensible. The pleasing noise reminded him of coolness, and he walked on out of the courtyard, through a wide stone doorway, and into a long and shady gallery, in either wall of which, both to north and south, was a series of magnificent windows that reached down from arched summits just below the ceiling to sills at the height of his waist, in all their depth framing nothing but blue sky. It appeared that just here the ridge narrowed and sharpened; for when he looked out to the north he seemed to be hanging directly over the sea; and similarly, to the south, it was as though a dropped stone would have plummeted straight down into the Mesaoria.

More like a cloister than a castle, he thought. What could this superb room have been? An ante-chamber, perhaps from which loiterers and petitioners might admire the view? But no, he thought; surely—it had to be—this was where the knights would have dined. Sitting on either side of a table which would have run almost the entire length of the gallery, they would have looked out of the windows into a sky which was somehow all the more immense for being framed, and then they would have risen, when the last of the Commanderia had been drained from the tankards, and looked down, either on to the spread chart of the terrain they were there to hold, or else on to the sea and then away beyond it to the land of the paynim, where Richard of England was riding under the Cross.

Fielding rested his bag on one of the broad window-sills and began to sort out his mid-day provisions. I too will dine here, he thought. I too will drink my wine where the castellans drank the sweet and heavy wine of Cyprus, and then dreamed of home.

Tom Llewyllyn and Gregory Stern were having lunch with Captain Detterling, who had arrived back in London the night before.

'So Fielding got a nasty shock,' Detterling was saying, 'the second inside a week, but he wasn't much hurt thanks to that homburg he was wearing. The Greeks were very apologetic. They explained that the matchet belonged to the sailor, who had lent it to our boatman, who was the sailor's uncle's wife's brother. The sailor was asking for it back, and the boatman wanted to keep it for another week, so they were having an argument ... at the end of which the boatman gave way and threw up the matchet. But just then the boat gave a lurch, the matchet was falling short, the sailor had to reach down too far and mistimed his swing ... etcetera, etcetera.'

'And what do you think?' said Tom. '*Was* it an accident?'

'Impossible to say. But of course Fielding's mind was made up anyhow. The business in Yugoslavia—that certainly hadn't been an accident, and it was that which had made him so determined to go ahead in the first place. And now here was this fellow Percival telling him just how to set about it—*and* saying that he'd probably be safer once he was in Cyprus, a judgment apparently confirmed when a sailor takes a shy at him with a rusty matchet. There was no holding Fielding after that. The very next morning he rang you up at the BBC and then took off for Cyprus. He didn't even wait to buy himself some more kit, though he'd only got the suit he stood up in. That was nearly a week ago, and I haven't heard a word from him since.'

'This man Percival,' said Gregory: 'is he to be relied on?'

'He plays a pretty sharp game of backgammon,' Detterling said, 'and Max de Freville thinks well of him.'

'What what about Max de Freville?' asked Tom.

'He's good at giving the right marks to men like Percival.'

'And this story of theirs ... about the American who called himself Diomedes?'

'If it's true,' said Detterling, 'it'll be worth every penny you're paying to get it.'

'I'd sooner have Fielding back home in one piece.'

'Amen to that,' Gregory said.

Both Tom and Gregory looked accusingly at Detterling. He had failed to offer them a ready-made solution; the ex-officer had let them down.

'Now you listen to me,' Detterling said. He drank off his port and put the glass down with a click. 'I asked Fielding, I urged him, to go back home. Since he refused to listen, since he was dead set on carrying on, I procured him the best advice I could about how to do so. Any complaints?'

This was too reasonable to be gainsaid. Gregory signed the bill and they all three departed, Tom to the Television Centre, Gregory and Detterling to the former's office, where they spent an acrid afternoon wrangling about Cavafy.

Fielding too had finished his food and wine. He put the remains of his meal back in his bag, then went to one of the windows in the south wall of the gallery. By craning his neck, he managed to get a view of his taxi, which was away below him to his left. The door was open and the driver's legs were sprawling out over the seat. Good. He had told the man he would eat and take his time up here, so that it would be a long while yet, even if the driver woke up, before his absence gave any cause for suspicion. There was no need to hurry. He picked up his bag, walked down the gallery and through another room, smaller and windowless, beyond it, and found, as he had expected, that there was a flight of steps leading down between two walls of stone to his right.

Somerset Lloyd-James and Lord Canteloupe were taking an afternoon walk in St James's Park.

'I've heard from the Director of Features at the BBC,' Somerset said. 'Some days ago, it seems, Fielding Gray rang up Tom Llewyllyn from Athens and said he was going straight on to Cyprus no matter what anyone said or did. He would hardly have acted with such precipitation unless he now has a definite lead.'

'Which might,' said Canteloupe, 'be *any* kind of lead.'

'Including the one kind which we don't want him to follow. If he *has* got on to that, then our Yankee friends are going to be very discommoded.'

'Serve them right. They should never have interfered in Cyprus in the first place.'

'But the point is,' said Somerset, 'that most of them haven't the faintest idea that they ever did interfere, and they'll be genuinely shocked when they find out. And what matters much more is that they're going to be made to look silly. Here, people will say, is the richest and most powerful government on earth, which is forever lecturing and hectoring the rest of us—and it doesn't even know what its own secret service is up to. This will be very irritating for the Americans, who will find some way of taking it out on us, although it isn't our fault. This in turn could be very damaging for the PM——'

'—Who will find some way of taking it out on me, although it isn't *my* fault.'

'Precisely.'

They paused on the iron bridge and looked down at the lake.

'Bloody ducks,' said Canteloupe, 'what do they care? It's all so unfair,' he went on crossly. 'This isn't a Fascist state. If the BBC sends a man to dig up the shit in Cyprus, what the hell can I do about it?'

'You are responsible to the Prime Minister,' said Somerset, 'for the suitable guidance of the popular media. If you fail, there are plenty of other people who will be glad of the place and the money.'

'*Bloody* ducks,' Canteloupe said.

'Of course,' said Somerset, 'I could have a word with Tom, but I hardly think he'd see the matter our way. He is very old-fashioned and still believes in publishing the truth, however manifestly inconvenient it may be. Whatever Fielding can prove, Tom will broadcast.'

'There's always this Director chappie. He seems ready to help. What sort of man is he?'

'He's a vegetarian,' said Somerset, 'and therefore a crank.

Like all cranks, he is self-important and obstinate. A little man, obsessed with his own rank ... which doesn't apply in this case, because Tom's been promised a free hand and only comes under the Director for administrative purposes.'

'He did what the Director asked about telling Gray to stay in Athens.'

'He was bound to listen to suggestions ... at first. But now Fielding's settled all that by taking off on his own.'

'Then it doesn't look as if either of them—either Llewyllyn or this Director—can be much use.'

They walked on towards the palace. Bellies and buttocks squirmed on the grass all round them. Lechery, thought Somerset: oestrus. Aloud he said:

'The Director, because he is a little man, knows the rules very well. The rules, you will remember, were originally drawn up by Lord Reith, a puritanical Scotsman who deprecated scandal among his employees.'

'Well?'

'Tom, although he is now respectably married, has a multi-coloured past. Now, it is just possible that his contract, as it extends over quite a long period, is governed by Reithian rules about correct moral behaviour, and that a public relapse into the habits of earlier days might disqualify him from his post. This much at least the Director will be able to tell us—the provisions of Tom's contract and the severity or otherwise with which these are currently enforced.'

'I see,' said Canteloupe. 'If the rules are still a bit stodgy——'

'—And if they were picturesquely contravened by Tom ... who, after all, has endured three years of marriage and might be grateful, given opportunity, for some light relief——'

'—Then he would be liable to dismissal——'

'—And it wouldn't matter so much where Fielding went or what he discovered——'

'—Because when he got back Llewyllyn would have gone, and no Llewyllyn, no programme. Very neat,' said Canteloupe; 'only what happens if he gets, say, the Billingsgate press to take his story instead of the BBC?'

'At least we've kept it off television. And Billingsgate talks the same language as we do.'

'Billingsgate,' said Canteloupe, 'is a counter-jumper from

the colonies.'

'He still talks our language. And now,' said Somerset, 'I must go and have a word or two in that language with the Director of Features.'

After going straight down for about twenty yards between walls on either side, the flight of steps which Fielding was descending emerged on to the open hillside, plunged steeply towards the sea for ten yards, and then swerved off to the left. Beyond this corner the steps continued some thirty yards further, now slanting gently across the slope between shallow banks covered with scrub; then they stopped, having deposited Fielding at the edge of a copse of fir-trees which grew out along a flat, wide spur. In the centre of the copse was a small open area, roughly circular and perhaps ten yards in diameter. Here Fielding put down his grip and carefully surveyed the scene in front of him.

'It is always said,' Max de Freville had told him, 'that the oldest Jewish cemetery surviving in Europe is in Worms. In fact it is at Castle Buffavento—if, that is, you can count Cyprus as being in Europe and a collection of three graves as a cemetery.'

And there they were: two square-topped head-stones, so deeply sunk that only three inches of either protruded above ground; and a long box-tomb, also sunk but still two feet in height and bearing, on the side which now faced him, an inscription in Hebrew characters.

'The Jew Elisha ben Habbakuk,' Max had said, 'made himself very useful to Richard I by lending him large sums of money while the king was on the island. Soon afterwards, when someone got up a nasty local programme in protest against current rates of interest, Elisha asked for help from Richard's followers and was given refuge, with his two daughters, up in Buffavento, which at that time was in English hands. All three were then murdered by the castle commander, who wanted the money Elisha brought with him, and buried just outside the precincts. The commander's knights, being offended by this treacherous behaviour, pushed the commander off the ramparts, announced that he had fallen when drunk, shared out Elisha's money between them and raised a subscription to put up decent tomb-stones where the old Jew and his daughters were buried. Even then, it seems, hypocrisy was a

British speciality.'

Fielding circled the box-tomb. He was not looking forward to what must come next.

'So much for the antiquarian background,' Leonard Percival had said. 'Now for some modern history. When the insurrection was at its worst, a Jewish–Greek schoolboy who was attending the Gymnasium at Nicosia accidentally learnt of a plan which some of his schoolfellows had made to blow up the local synagogue in protest against the neutralist attitude of the Jews in Cyprus. The boy informed the police of the plan and the incendiaries were caught in the act. Now, it was not at all unusual, as you will certainly remember, for school-children to chuck explosives about, but what was very unusual indeed was that someone should have dared to inform against them. Since that someone was obviously a Jew, and since there were very few Jews at the Gymnasium, they soon found out who had gone to the police, and Diomedes decided that a particularly striking example must be made, in order to deter other would-be delators. In fact he had the boy killed by the old-fashioned method of bending back two springy young trees, tying one of the boy's ankles to the top of each, and then letting the trees go ... This on the edge of the main road from Kyrenia into Nicosia, with a large notice set up to inform passers-by that this was what DIOMEDES OF EOKA had in store for anyone who failed to mind his own business. It was improbable that the police would allow this exhibit to stay there for long, but it was thought that enough people would see it at daybreak for the world at large to get the message.

'But as it happened, the police were on the scene only just too late to rescue the boy and in time to cut down his remains before anyone at all had seen them. There was then a swift consultation, which ended in rather a surprising decision. The point was, you see, that although this very ugly murder could have been used to stir up indignation against EOKA, there was also no doubt that if it were made public it would have just the effect Diomedes wanted it to have— of deterring all informers whatever from then on. Since there were few enough of them as it was, this would have been most unhelpful for the authorities. It was therefore decided to hush up the whole business and hide the body—if that's what it could still be called—so securely that no one would ever see it or make any kind of report on its condition.'

'How do you know all this?' Fielding had asked.

'I was there when the boy was found ... Even in these circumstances, however, good old British hypocrisy was in evidence: as much respect as possible must be had for the corpse. So since the boy was half Jewish, and since someone knew of this burial ground up at Buffavento, the body was whipped away up to the castle, where it would be right out of everyone's way but lying in ground that was more or less hallowed in its associations. The whole thing had to be done there and then and before it got light, without giving anyone a chance to know what was happening, so there was no time to make a coffin; and the most respectful thing to do—or so it seemed to the chap in charge—was to place the corpse in the hollow tomb which the knights had set up over old Elisha. So that was what they did ... and drove back down the mountain some hours later, as though they were returning from a routine patrol, and nobody any the wiser.'

For some time, as he stood by the box-tomb, Fielding considered the Hebrew lettering. Although it was meaningless to him, its cabbalistic apparatus gave it a weird significance: such mysterious characters, he felt, must surely spell out a prayer or rune of the most powerful kind, perhaps a curse on any man who dared to disturb the grave.

He went back to his bag and took out a chisel and a small metal lever.

'You should not find it difficult,' Percival had said, 'to shift the slab on top. Though I'm told the police had quite a job of it...'

Fielding inserted the chisel under the overlapping edge of the slab. He pressed the handle down and felt the slab lift very slightly; with his other hand he pushed the lever in beside the chisel.

'It was careless of me,' Percival had told him when instructing him what to look for: 'I should have taken it off the boy's remains as soon as we found him. But there were so many things to think about and just then it didn't seem important. All this happened, you understand, before I had really begun to equate Diomedes with my old colleague Restarick. It was only much later on, after I had left the island, that I finally became sure of this, and it was then I remembered what had been on that wretched boy's body. It went with him when they drove him away up the mountain. It *must* be there with him still.'

Fielding tested the lever. He would prise up the slab about six inches, he decided, get one hand underneath it and then the other (releasing the lever as he did so), and push the slab over until the far edge tilted to the ground. That should leave me plenty of room, he thought. Here goes.

Six seconds later he reeled back from the tomb and stumbled away to the trees, trembling helplessly and emitting great gouts of vomit. Gradually, however, he became calmer. At length he went to his bag, took out a bottle of water, dampened his handkerchief and tied it over his mouth and nose, making a knot behind his head. Then he went back to the tomb and looked firmly and steadily down. Yes; that must be it—if Percival was right. He leant forward, put both hands down and round the neck, and began to fumble.

'Restarick/Diomedes,' Percival had said, 'isn't really a cruel man. He wouldn't have wanted to cause avoidable pain—not under his own nose. He would have been quite content with leaving the impression—such a very horrible impression—that pain had been caused. Furthermore, he would not have wanted noise or struggle. So what more natural than that he should have chloroformed the boy before he killed him? Or killed him *first* with chloroform? In the car on the way, perhaps. He would have soaked a handkerchief in chloroform to make a pad, held it to the boy's face until he ceased to struggle, and then, wanting to make quite sure but also to leave his own hands free to handle ropes and torches and the rest, he would have secured the pad to the boy's face with a second handkerchief, tied like a mask. Something like that. It must have been.'

'How can you possibly know?'

'Because there was a handkerchief tied round the boy's neck when we found him. I didn't take much notice, I thought it was the boy's own, which he had been sporting as some kind of neckwear. It was only years later, when I was finally sure that Restarick was Diomedes, that I remembered two things about that handkerchief. First, the knot was at the back of the neck—as though the handkerchief had been fastened round the face and then slipped down,

And secondly, it had been immaculately clean and of very fine linen. Not at all the sort of handkerchief usually owned by sixth-formers from the Nicosia Gymnasium—though I was much too preoccupied and upset to think of that at the time. You see, the whole body, right up to the chest ... was bisected.'

Desperately, Fielding's fingers now clawed at the knot, which he had worked round to one side of the neck. Gangrene, he thought; people who muck about with dead bodies get their blood poisoned, it's always happening to students, the tiniest cut or flaw in the skin and the infection seeps through ...

'Now, one of the things about Restarick,' Percival had said, 'is that he's rather a dandy. He had beautiful suits. And he used to have all his personal linen specially made up by a firm in Dover Street—like all Americans, he greatly admired British clothes. And so if, as I'm sure, the handkerchief round that poor little Jew's neck was Restarick's——'

'—Then the firm in Dover Street will be able to identify it?'

'Very easily. On all his shirts and handkerchiefs and the rest he used to have his personal mark embroidered, like a kind of crest. A Maltese Cross.'

Fielding's sweaty fingers trembled and slipped. His hand touched the neck and his throat heaved. With a great effort he mastered himself and once more tackled the knot. Could any mere handkerchief be worth such torture?

'Surely,' he remembered saying to Percival, 'he'd never have left such a conspicuous object behind him on that boy's body?'

'I've no doubt he had every intention of removing it. But it didn't work out as he thought ... They arrive at the scene of execution and carry the body from the car. All in total darkness. They bend back the trees, which they have selected earlier by daylight. Two men secure them. Another man busies himself with the boy's ankles. Meanwhile Restarick pulls the pad out from under the mask and starts to untie the mask itself. The knot is tight and it won't undo. Someone blunders or panics, the trees are released before Restarick is ready ... Then, when it's all over, he hears a car in the distance: the police. Hurriedly he tears at the knot in the handkerchief—standing on his toes, perhaps, because the parting trees have swung the body well clear. So he reaches up for the hanging head, and he can't risk a torch, and the car is getting closer. One final attempt to drag the handkerchief off the head, but it's tightly tied and he can't see and he's sweating with fear—so he runs for it with the rest of his men and hopes for the best.'

'Guesswork. All of it.'

'All except for one handkerchief of finest quality linen...'

This handkerchief, Fielding thought now. The knot too tight to undo. '... One final attempt to drag the handkerchief off...' Too tightly tied even for that ... then ... But now ... There is ... something different ... now. Slowly he peeled the linen up over the poor sunken face; clearly visible, amid the stains on the underside, was a Maltese Cross embroidered in green. The handkerchief stuck slightly and he gave a quick pull. The handkerchief came away and his knuckles rapped very sharply against the inside of the tomb. *Cuts; flaws in the skin.* Weeping with terror he threw down the cerement and ran for his bag. He scrabbled in it for the wine bottle, poured the lees over his knuckles, rubbed them well in. Would it be strong enough to disinfect? He must get back to Nicosia and find a doctor in case. But first there were things he must do. Still pouring with tears, he removed his own handkerchief from his face, dropped it on top of the filthy thing on the ground, gathered them up together and thrust them into his bag. Then he went back to the tomb to work the slab into its proper position. But no, he thought, there's something else I must do first, what is it, O God, what is it? Yes. *Yes.*

He felt in his breast pocket and took out the Mezuzah. Gregory won't mind, he thought, as he placed it on the broken body.

'Forgive me,' he cried out loud as the tears of terror and pity and disgust streamed off his cheeks, 'please forgive me. Don't let there be a curse. Let the sacred name of Shaddai absolve me from your curse.'

Part 2: Arcadia

'I'm sorry,' said Tom Llewyllyn to Fielding Gray in the Television Centre, 'but it simply isn't enough.'

'I quite agree.'

'All you've produced,' continued Tom, 'is one handkerchief which you found round the neck of a corpse. True, you have been able to verify that it was sold to this man Restarick by a London firm of haberdashers; but what does that prove? Handkerchiefs are easily lost or stolen. Even if you can show that Restarick was in Cyprus at the time of the murder, that handkerchief does not necessarily prove that he was present at the killing, or that he was helping EOKA, or that he was Diomedes.'

'But it does create a strong supposition that he was mixed up in it all somewhere?'

'In this sort of case we can't afford to deal in suppositions.'

'I have already said that I agree.'

'Then why,' said Tom, 'have you come back to London so soon? Not but what I'm very pleased to see you.'

'I've come back,' said Fielding, 'to make quite certain where I stand. There have already been signs—that telegram to Athens—that the BBC isn't over-enthusiastic about this enquiry, and I don't imagine that the implications of what I *have* discovered will give very much pleasure. And so I want your assurance that if I follow this through, whatever I later discover will be fully and fairly presented on television and not suppressed or laughed off.'

'I'm in sole charge,' said Tom, 'of Today is History. You have my assurance—you always had it—that I will broadcast anything of value which you may discover in or about Cyprus. But are you sure you want to go back? Haven't you had enough trouble already?'

'Look,' said Fielding. 'I have persisted so far in order to find out the truth for myself. This I have now done to my own broad satisfaction, but, as we both agree, I have not yet come up with enough solid evidence to justify making the matter public. Since I think the matter should be made public, I am prepared to go back and hunt for more evidence, however disagreeable the circumstances, provided that

I am assured of your support——'

'—Which you are——'

'—And also that you will now define exactly what sort of proof you will require from me before going ahead with an exposé.'

Tom put his hands in his hair and his elbows on his desk. His eye was promptly caught by a large piece of paper which bore the memo *Call for Baby's Cod-Liver Oil and Malt*, an instruction which had been telephoned by Patricia just before Fielding arrived. He shuddered with irritation and re-addressed himself, not without effort, to the affair in hand.

'Difficult,' he said. 'What do you think you can offer?'

'My informant, Percival,' Fielding said, 'who was dead right about that handkerchief, has now come up with something else.' Leonard Percival had in fact emerged from wherever he had been lurking to meet Fielding at London Airport the previous evening. In the taxi from the airport to Buttock's Hotel he had expressed satisfaction at what Fielding had achieved and issued crisp instructions for the next move. 'Something else,' Fielding said now, 'of a rather different kind.'

'Well?'

Fielding rose and went to the window which looked down on the White City Stadium. Tom, he thought, is not going to like this. Well, supposing he doesn't? I can just give the whole thing up, and that will be that. I've done what I wanted to; I've defied those who tried to bully me and found out the truth which they wished to hide; my honour is satisfied. I've won the game and I know it, and I'm surely a mature enough man not to care whether or not the result is made public.

And yet he knew very well that he did care. He cared, not on grounds of morality or politics or patriotism, but simply because he had an intense personal distaste for agitators—for all people like Restarick who (whatever their motives) went round stirring up trouble where there had been peace and quiet before. Such people made everything they came near ugly and uncomfortable. He, Fielding, resented them, he wanted them caught and humiliated and put out of the way. Until recently his hatred had been all for the Cypriots, who had taken one of his eyes and ruined his face for ever; but now, now that he knew what he did, it was Restarick he

wanted to punish, not so much because Restarick was ultimately responsible for the events which had led to his dis-
figurement, as because Restarick was representative of those
forces of disruption which were daily posing a more vicious
threat to all the things he cherished.

For Restarick was the Enemy: he stood for Change. To
be sure, he was the agent of an American organisation
which existed to promote stability and good order through-
out the world; but in this instance that organisation, in-
spired by jealousy of Empire, by sheer atavistic spite, was
following a deliberate policy of rabble-rousing and revolu-
tion. Restarick had been sent to Cyprus to play the dema-
gogue, to inflate trivial discontent to the point of obscene
explosion. Restarick stood for disintegration, he stood for
rant, for 'protest', for subversion—and Restarick must be
destroyed. Which meant that Restarick must be exposed; so
that it was very important, as Fielding now recognised, that
he should not give up at this stage, that he should persevere
until he could bring a public case. For this he needed Tom's
support; but Tom, he knew, would not be pleased when
Fielding told him what must come next, and it would have
to be put to him with care.

'Well?' Tom said.

'According to Percival,' said Fielding, 'there was a large
notice left behind near that Jewish boy who was murdered.
This specifically stated that it was Diomedes—not Dighenis,
which was what Grivas called himself, but *Diomedes*—who
had engineered this act of revenge. Never mind whether or
not he was actually there, it was Diomedes who had given
that order, and someone was evidently anxious that people
should know this was the case. Now, who and why?'

'Perhaps Dighenis—i.e. Grivas—wanted to dissociate
himself?'

'Precisely. Diomedes was making a stern and necessary
example, as he thought, but Grivas reckoned that this particular piece of atrocity was going too far and would probably do harm to his reputation. This fits in very well with
your "Grivas was just a decent soldier" theory. He couldn't
prevent Diomedes, if only because Diomedes was the agent
of those who were providing the cash, but he wasn't going
to be held personally responsible for *this* bit of beastliness.
And so with or without Diomedes' knowledge, Grivas
arranged for a notice to be left behind saying that it was all

Diomedes' work.'

'You're still no nearer proving who Diomedes was.'

'Wait a little ... Now, in the event it didn't matter what the notice said because the mess was cleared away by the police before anyone knew about it. In fact, the whole thing was so carefully hushed up that only a handful of people know about it even to this day.'

'All right. But where does all this get you?'

'It gets me to Athens. It gets me to the house of General Grivas, as he is now styled, telling him how much, as an ex-soldier myself, I admire his conduct of the campaign in Cyprus. True, I shall say, the terrorist element was unfortunate, but after all Grivas was outnumbered and had no choice. In the circumstances, he could be forgiven a few dead civilians, a few bombs in the markets and the taverns, because it was the only way to make his point. Indeed, I shall tell him, it is now generally agreed that the whole affair does him nothing but credit. So much so that BBC Television is very keen to do a piece about it—a piece which will demonstrate, in typical breast-tearing English fashion, that everything was all our fault and that our enemies were the most spotless and courageous of idealists.'

'Go on,' said Tom, frowning down at the memo about Baby's Malt.

'Well,' said Fielding, 'Grivas will sit there purring, and I shall then ask permission to put a few preliminary questions. Because, I shall say, there is one slight snag. Our investigations have revealed that there was one very nasty piece of work indeed, which up till now nobody knows about. The barbarous mutilation of a young Jewish boy, who was literally torn apart. No doubt about it: if necessary we can produce the body. Impersonal terrorism is one thing, I shall proceed, but this is quite another. Will the General kindly explain?'

'Oh yes, yes, the General can explain: that particular murder was done against his wishes—he even had a notice put up to disown it. "I'm afraid, sir, that I must ask you to be more precise." Very well: it was arranged by his—er—assistant, Diomedes. "And who was he?" Well, er ... "Come come, General. Diomedes is just a code-name. It could mean anybody or nobody. Who was he? What was his role? Because if you don't tell me, the BBC will have to take a less tolerant view of your activities. I shall be compelled to report that I have inspected the remains of a victim—a mere child—whose manner of death was more revolting than anything since Dachau, and for whose murder General Grivas himself must be held responsible." And what, Tom, does this gallant officer do then? Does he sit there and endure the stain on his honour? Or does he come up with the truth about Restarick?'

'He kicks you straight out of the house,' said Tom, 'if, indeed, he ever let you into it. I don't like it, Fielding. I don't like the way you propose to use threats in the name of the BBC——'

'—You can always say I exceeded my brief——'

'—And leaving that aside, I just don't care for your method. It's sheer blackmail—against all conscience.'

'It's only *my* conscience that need be involved. Leave that to me.'

'*I* shall be responsible for using the stuff.'

'But not for getting it. You need know nothing more that.'

'You've already told me what you intend.'

'Pure speculation, dear boy. An imaginative version of the way things just might work out. Look, Tom,' said Fielding, 'what it boils down to is this: if I come back from Athens, bringing a signed statement from Grivas, or some other authoritative figure in this field, that Diomedes was the American, Earle Restarick, will you accept it as evidence?'

Tom breathed heavily and clenched both fists.

'Yes,' he said at last: 'if you can prove the signature.'

'What about a tape recording?'

'Yes; if Grivas or whoever gives it his written attestation.'

'And suppose I get the recording without his knowing?'

'Then I shall require one other witness, besides yourself, to swear that the tape is genuine.'

'Fair enough,' said Fielding. 'So those are your conditions and you will stand by them?'

'I will,' said Tom, wiping his palms on his lapels.

'Good,' said Fielding. 'I shall leave for Athens as soon as you send me an air ticket. First class, please.'

'My budget isn't bottomless.'

'It'll run to first-class air tickets for old friends. I shall be at Tessie Buttock's.'

'Oh, all right,' said Tom, and ground his teeth. 'Give my love to Tessie.'

'Tom sends his love,' said Fielding to Tessie Buttock that evening.

'There's a dear boy, like he always was. How was he looking?'

'A bit harassed. I think this BBC job worries him.'

'I hope,' said Tessie, 'that wife of his is feeding him proper.'

'I doubt it. She was used to a big house in the country with plenty of servants. She hasn't taken to London.'

'She could learn. I've no patience with these girls that put on airs.'

'It's not altogether her fault,' said Fielding. 'For years now Tom has been making a lot of money, and he could easily afford a house or a large flat with a girl to live in and help with the work and the baby. Instead of which he insists on living in a poky little hole in Southwell Gardens and won't have a servant anywhere near the place. Something to do with his socialist conscience.'

'But even socialists have servants,' Tessie said. 'Anyway, Tom was always in and out of restaurants, and he had people waiting on him when he lived here.'

'Hotels and restaurants are different. You pay an agreed sum for an agreed service. But if you have servants in your own home, Tom told me once, it sets up a feudal relationship which is a denial of human dignity on both sides. His own words.'

'What rubbish. Ask Albert Edward,' Tessie said, and poked the snoring dog. 'A fat lot he cares for his human dignity as long as he's warm and fed.'

'I also think,' said Fielding, 'that consciously or not Tom's punishing Patricia for having had a rich and easy childhood. Whereas he himself—well, no one even knows where he came from.'

'He once told me something,' Tessie said, 'which made me think his mother must have had a rough time. "Four of us," he said, "and she could never be sure the money would come." So perhaps he's punishing this Patricia because of his mother.'

'Or perhaps he's sending his mother a lot of money to make up and can't afford anything better than Southwell Gardens after all. Anyway, the long and the short of it is that he's turning Patricia into a drudge and seems to regard it as the natural fate for a married woman.' Fielding disengaged his thigh from the embrace of Albert Edward and rose from the fender-cushion. 'So long, Tessie. I'm off out.'

'Not staying in for supper, dear? I've got your favourite steak and kidney.'

'Sorry, love. I've got a date.'

'Made it with my own hands.'

'Never mind,' said Fielding, who knew as well as Tessie did that it had come out of a tin, 'it'll make a nice treat for Albert Edward.'

'I can't imagine,' said Patricia Llewyllyn in Southwell Gardens, 'what made you forget Baby's Cod-Liver Oil and Malt.'

'I've had a difficult day,' said Tom, 'and I had more important things to remember. Anyway, why couldn't you get it?'

'Baby and I went to see Isobel, which is the wrong way for the chemist.'

'How was Isobel?'

'Very energetic. She was cleaning out the attic.'

'Why not follow her example?'

'We haven't got an attic.'

'We've got a sitting-room,' said Tom, looking despondently round it.

'Somehow,' said Patricia, 'I can't bring myself to care much about it. It's such a transitory kind of place. Now, Isobel and Gregory's house——'

'—Is all very well for Isobel and Gregory. I'm different. I've always lived in transitory places. I couldn't do anything else.'

'What about me?' said Patricia.

'Come over here,' said Tom.

When Patricia came to him, he took her on his knee and kissed her on the lips.

'Remember what I told you when we were married?' he said.

'Tom ... Kiss me again.'

'In a minute ... Remember I said that I was a writer before I was a husband? And that in some ways my writing would always have to come first?'

'Yes.'

'Well, this flat,' said Tom, 'is one of those ways. A writer is someone who lives in passage, and so this flat is just a place of passage. Soon we shall move to another. We shall never have a house like Isobel and Gregory, not even if I make a million pounds, until I am dead as a writer. Do you understand?'

'I think so. Tom, Baby's asleep. Come with me.'

Later on, while they were eating Heinz Spaghetti on toast, Tom said:

'Have you seen my National Insurance Card? They keep asking for it at the BBC.'

'I don't think you've ever had one.'

'But I thought they came automatically.'

'You have to stamp them,' Patricia explained, 'and send them in at the beginning of every March, and then they send you another one for the next year. If you've never had one, you'll never get one ... if you see what I mean.'

'Have you got one?'

'Oh yes. That typist woman of Daddy's used to stamp them for all of us. I suppose she still does.'

'But not for me?'

'Of course not, darling. Unless you gave her yours when we got married?'

'No. As you say, I don't think I've ever had one. No one's ever asked for it before.'

'They don't, unless you take a job.'

'But surely,' said Tom, getting rather worked-up, 'they ought to have sent me one when the whole business started. I mean, I'm a citizen, I'm *entitled* to a National Insurance Card.'

'Darling, darling Tom,' said Patricia, 'you have such funny ideas about the Welfare State. *They* don't send you anything. *You* have to go and apply for it.'

'Well, they must realise after all this time that I haven't got one.'

'Not,' said Patricia, 'if you're a writer who lives in passage. You've never given them a chance to catch up with you.'

'Come to think of it,' said Tom, 'when I was living at Tessie Buttock's, I did have an official letter one day, but I never even saw it. Tessie read it—she read all the letters—and then wrote "Not known at this address" on the envelope and popped it back in the box. She told me about it later. You don't want to be bothered with muck like that, she said.'

'Tom, darling,' said Patricia cautiously, 'you *do* pay income tax?'

'Of course,' said Tom severely. 'It's my plain social duty. Gregory employs an accountant for me and they deduct it from my royalties as they fall due.'

'Well, that's a relief. I wouldn't want you to go to prison. But this other thing—what are you going to tell the BBC?'

Tom thought for a moment.

'I'll tell them,' he said, 'that I gave my card to you to get it stamped for me and that Baby went and tore it up. Then they can go ahead and apply for a new one. There's always a simple answer to this sort of nonsense.'

Patricia giggled with sheer love.

'I can't help feeling,' she said, 'that someone will want to be told just a tiny bit more than that.'

'Well, dearie,' Maisie said to Fielding, 'you *have* learnt a thing or two since you've been away. One of those dirty foreign girls, was it?'

'An old acquaintance, as it happens. Someone I met quite by accident.'

'She ought to be ashamed of herself, showing you things like that. Old acquaintance, indeed. You were more than acquainted by the time you got through that little lot.'

'It was rather revealing.'

'Well, I hope *you* didn't do any revealing,' Maisie said. 'Remember what I told you before. Don't let on what's going on in there.' She scratched the hairs on his chest. 'Not when you're dealing with that kind of person. You never know who'll hear about it next.'

'Not to worry,' Fielding told her. 'We only talked about things which happened a very long time ago.'

'Old acquaintances met again by accident,' Maisie said, 'can be the most dangerous people of all. You start thinking you're young again, like you were when you first knew them, and there's no end to the silliness that goes on.'

'Harmless silliness. And very delightful.'

'That's as may be. Start behaving as though you're young all over again, and the next thing you know you've gone and ruptured a blood vessel ... So you're off back there in a day or two?'

'That's right.'

'Well, you watch out for old acquaintances,' said Maisie; 'particularly if they start teaching you new tricks.'

Angela Tuck, though she had too much sense to mourn long for departed lovers, would often wonder curiously what had become of this one or that. About Fielding Gray, after their brief encounter on Hydra, she pondered the more as there were several unusual items to add spice. These included their somewhat lurid connection in the distant past, the much talked of incident which had taken place while Fielding was boarding the steamer for Athens, and the strong impression she had otherwise received that he and Detterling were up to something on the sly. It also occurred to her, although she was not a book-loving woman, that it might be interesting to read the novels which Fielding had written.

When, therefore, she was passing through Athens a few days later (*en route* with Max for Cyprus) she called in at the large bookshop off Constitution Square and was impressed to find that all three of Fielding's novels were in stock. (She would have been less impressed had she known that they were the only copies in Greece, having been ordered by an English resident who had since been hurriedly repatriated.) After she and Max had established themselves in Cyprus at the Dome Hotel in Kyrenia, she was faced with two days' solitude (while Max moved hither and thither seeking preliminary reactions to his proposals for a casino on the island) and so had the ideal opportunity for a good, long read. She therefore sought out her glasses, sat down on the English-style terrace overlooking the sea, ordered a bottle of sweet white wine, and then, having in some respects a very tidy nature, examined the three books to find out in what order they had been written and started in on page one of the first.

This she found of little interest. It was, she fancied, rather well written, but it also struck her as being frigid and superior in tone. Furthermore, it was concerned with the exclusively male world of the British Army on active service and came to a climax during an elaborate court martial, a form of proceeding which she regarded as pompous and absurd. As it happened, she had spent much of her own childhood and adolescence in military circles in India with a father who was later court-martialled for embezzlement, but this period of her life, which had ended abruptly with her father's dismissal, she considered as so irrelevant to her more recent destinies that she had scarcely given it a single thought in the last ten years. She was certainly not prepared to revive memories of it now in order to assist her appreciation of Fielding's novel—the scene of which, in any case, was set not in India but in East Africa.

The second book was rather more to her taste. It had to do with a native tribe, which was starving to death because the only food available was forbidden to it for religious reasons, and with the efforts of a young colonial officer, first to overcome the tribe's scruples, then to trick it into eating the prohibited meat. The problem was made real for her and the solution was ingenious; but once again the interest was largely professional, there wasn't a woman in sight, and the writing was so contemptuous of human folly and ignorance that she felt herself, along with all mankind, to have been viciously insulted. After this, she had almost decided not to bother with the third book at all—until a cursory inspection of the blurb made her open her eyes wider than she had opened them in some weeks and sent her back to work with a will.

Fielding Gray's third and most recent novel, published only a few months before, was called *Love's Jest Book*. As Angela had gathered from her glance at the blurb, the material was autobiographical and was drawn, what was more, from that period of Fielding's life when she herself had first known him: it embraced all the subjects and events which they had discussed on that memorable afternoon in Angela's bed on Hydra, and a great many more besides. Having opened with an account of how the hero (Fielding to the life) had fallen in love at his school with a fair and well-made boy called Alexis, the book went on to relate how Alexis was seduced and then deserted; how he sought consolation, was arrested by the police and was consigned to the care of a psychiatrist; and how finally, after a further and even more brutal exhibition of the Fielding-hero's treachery, he had blown his brains out with his father's revolver.

This was the central story. But there were also several passages about Angela herself, most notably those which described her liaison with the adolescent Somerset Lloyd-James (thinly disguised under the name of William Glyn-

Davies) and the part later played by Somerset and herself in bringing about Fielding's exposure and disgrace. All of this Angela found fascinating. From noon until tea-time of the second day of Max's absence she sat on the hotel terrace absorbed in this violently romantic but (as she herself could vouch) substantially true tale of love and betrayal and death; and when she finally closed the book, she felt that Fielding's art had done justice to his matter.

'Clever,' she mused to herself as she crossed the terrace to go indoors, 'very clever. But it's more than that. He's obsessed. Even now, all these years later, he's obsessed.'

'So,' said Leonard Percival: 'you know where to send to me if you've got any news?'

Percival was seeing Fielding off on the aeroplane from London to Athens.

'American Express, Rome,' said Fielding. 'And if I'm in trouble in Athens, I'm to go to 236a, Philhellene Street.'

'Right. Though for the reasons I've explained to you, I think that from now on any pressures on you will be oblique. Not to be avoided, that is, merely by going to ground in Philhellene Street. Next point. You've got your story absolutely straight—the one you're going to use for getting an interview with Grivas?'

'Yes. Whatever he may have heard, I shall say, I've been misunderstood. Despite what happened to me personally during the Cyprus campaign, I'm not after making trouble. I admire his strategy and I want to make a sympathetic study of it ... not only for the BBC but for publication as a book. I shall write to him and say just that the moment I get to Athens.'

'Good. Although he'll have been firmly warned against you, it might just work. Grivas dislikes being bossed about, by Restarick or anyone else, and the idea of meeting a man who fought against him in the field will appeal to the romantic side in him. Old enemies discussing past battles over a drink—like a scene from John Buchan. Grivas is quite innocent enough, quite old-fashioned enough to go for the idea.'

'And if he doesn't?'

'Then you'll have to consider ways and means of breaking in on him, and either charming him or forcing him into giving you a hearing.'

'If it comes to that, I'll need help.'

'If it comes to that, you shall have it.'

Fielding's flight was called on the loud-speaker.

'Time to take wing,' said Percival: 'don't fly too near the sun.'

Earle Restarick, dressed in black silk pyjamas and a white silk scarf, was drinking coffee in the sitting-room of a villa above Bellapaix. The villa, which had once been a small monastery, could only be reached by a mule-track. From where Restarick sat, he looked straight along the track, which descended a gentle slope for about quarter of a mile and then dipped sharply out of sight down the hill-side. Restarick's eye, taking off from this point like a ski-jumper, hovered in the sky a moment and then dropped towards the Abbey of Bellapaix, hovered again, and then swept down through the foot-hills to the fort by Kyrenia harbour. He gave a long sigh of pleasure and turned unwillingly to the Greek Cypriot who was standing beside him.

'And then?' Restarick said.

'And then he told me to take him to Buffavento. At Buffavento he looked round and ate his lunch and told me to take him back again. Just another day's sight-seeing. The next morning I took him to Nicosia airport, where he caught the plane for Londino.'

'Had he told you before that he was leaving?'

'He never told me anything. Only where to drive him. Otherwise he hardly spoke.'

'But he was polite?' said Restarick.

'Yes.'

'And generous with his tips?'

'Yes'—reluctantly.

'Then you have nothing to complain of.'

'Except that he regarded me as just a part of the taxi. An important part, but otherwise no different from the rest of it.'

'The English,' said Restarick, 'like to pay their own way and keep their own council. They do not understand that those whom they are paying expect to be treated as equals.'

'But you Americans are different,' said the Cypriot in a flurry of sycophancy; 'you believe in human brotherhood.'

'There is nevertheless a lot to be said,' remarked Restarick, 'for the English point of view. Here is your money.'

The Cypriot counted it carefully.

'But this morning,' he said, 'I have been away from my taxi. And now I must walk back down that accursed mule-track. All that time it takes, kyrios, all that time.'

'If you snivel like that,' said Restarick, 'even we Americans will find it hard to regard you as a brother.'

The man held out two hands towards him, but Restarick left his chair and walked out of the room without paying any further attention. He went down a passage and turned into a small study. At a desk by the window, which looked straight into the hill-side as it rose from the back of the villa, a stocky man with close-cut hair was fiddling with the insides of a short-range radio transmitter. Behind him, against one wall, was a much bigger one, and fastened to the wall beside it a large-scale map of the island.

'I've just checked by telephone with Athens,' the stocky man said. 'Gray arrived by plane from London last night.'

'Thank you, Savidis. And I've been talking with that taxi-driver. He insists that Gray merely went sight-seeing here in Cyprus and then just left. If he drew a blank here, why should he be returning to Athens?'

Savidis shrugged.

'The BBC are paying him well. Perhaps he's persuaded them to let him have another try.'

'But why did he go back to London at all? The BBC didn't send for him.'

Savidis shrugged again.

'We must assume,' said Restarick, 'that he's on to something, something big enough to take him back to London for advice. Since he's been in touch with Leonard Percival, that's only too likely to be true. I've no idea how much Leonard knows, but he must know something, and the bastard's out to do us down. We've been squeezing the English service out of Europe and the Near East for years now, and even where they're still in the game nine times out of ten we've been first to find the honey-pot. But if they could get us publicly discredited over Cyprus, Washington might get nervous and call off some of our other Mediterranean activities, and then Percival and his buddies would have a fair chance to get back their old influence in their old stamping grounds.'

'Can England still afford that sort of influence?'

'I wouldn't know. What I *do* know is that the British Government doesn't want any revelations about Cyprus because it doesn't want anyone to realise that we've made a fool of it, and it's therefore instructed Percival's branch, very firmly, to forget the whole affair. But that won't stop Percival's bosses—with their greedy eyes on our territory—if they can see a way round. And what better way round than using this man Gray to do the dirty work and dish it all up on television? That way, Leonard and his crowd would get everything they wanted—*and* they could tell their Government in London that they'd obeyed their instructions and kept out of it themselves. Go and complain to the BBC, they could say; it's this BBC man who's come out with it all, no good blaming us.'

'All right,' said Savidis. 'It fits. So what do we do?'

'We hope,' said Restarick, 'that the British authorities will keep a sharp eye on the BBC and stop Gray broadcasting anything which either they or we wouldn't like.'

'But we can't rely on this. We never could. Which is why it was decided to kill Gray at the very beginning—just in case, we said.'

'Only both attempts were unfortunately bungled by your fellow-countrymen.'

'I've been a naturalised American,' said Savidis, 'for twenty-five years. I agree in advance with anything you may care to say about the incompetence both of Greeks in general and of Cypriot Greeks in particular. Let us now revert to my point, which is simply this: if there was good enough reason to get rid of Gray "just in case" before he even arrived here, there is far, far better reason now that he's apparently getting hot.'

'Granted,' said Restarick, removing his scarf as he spoke; 'the only trouble is that it's now too late.'

'Surely not.'

'From the moment he arrived in Cyprus it was too late. Once he was here, the connection would have been too obvious. We all agreed about that.'

'I know. But he's not in Cyprus now, he's in Athens.'

'Meanwhile he's been back to London,' Restarick said. He refolded his scarf and started to ease it back round his neck and under his pyjama collar. 'He's reported to the BBC on his progress, which means, very probably, that he's had something to say about us. If we kill him now—whether in Athens or Timbuktu—his death will at once be imputed to us and his discoveries to date will get all the publicity Percival could ever have dreamed of.'

'If Gray had proper proof,' said Savidis, 'he wouldn't have needed to come back. Since he hasn't got proper proof, he cannot have told the BBC anything *definite* about us, and therefore nothing definite can come out after his death. Provided it occurs *now*.'

'Enough would come out to compel us to keep very quiet while the fuss was dying down. We're a long way from being finished here and we can't afford that kind of delay. No,' said Restarick, making a final adjustment to his scarf; 'Fielding Gray stays alive.'

'And dangerous.'

'Yes,' mused Restarick. 'Dangerous because intelligent. Dangerous because inquisitive. How does one stop a man being intelligent and inquisitive without actually killing him? Always an amusing problem.'

He examined the map on the wall and sang a little song to himself, a song that had been popular just after the war.

> '*Though it's only a cardboard moon,*' he sang,
> '*Sailing over a painted sea,*
> *Though it's only make-believe . . .*
> *. . . Di-dee, di-dee, di-dee.*'

'Forgotten the last line?' said Savidis.

'Yes. But the first three will suffice for our purpose. The Widow Tuck,' he said, swinging round on his companion. 'She's come here from Hydra with de Freville, we hear, and they're staying at the Dome Hotel down in Kyrenia?'

'Right. But what's she got to do with it?'

'The sailor folk on Hydra report that while Gray was there she spent a very long afternoon in bed with him.'

'Ah, I see,' said Savidis sarcastically. 'We send the woman Tuck off to Athens, and tell her to go to bed with Major Gray and never let him get up? Until he dies of fornication, maybe?'

'For all your twenty-five years as an American citizen,' Restarick said, 'you still think like a Balkan peasant.'

'And you think like a eunuch. Why not kill him and be done?'

'Eunuchs ruled Byzantium rather effectively for nearly a thousand years, Savidis. Do try to remember your own history.'

'I live in the present.'

'Like all peasants.' Earle Restarick passed his fingers over the delicately embroidered Maltese Cross on his scarf. 'Well,' he said, 'you have your uses, I suppose. You can demonstrate your efficacy in the present, my dear Savidis, by going into Kyrenia forthwith and discreetly making the following arrangements for the entertainment of Madame Tuck...'

6: Revivals

'Maisie,' said Somerset Lloyd-James. 'We'll get her.'

'Who's Maisie?' said Lord Canteloupe.

'An old friend...'

'I still don't understand.'

'Then have some more of this nice claret and listen carefully.'

They were lunching at the Ritz, largely because this was about the only place left in London where the tables were still far enough apart for the occupants to converse unheard. Although Canteloupe was paying for the lunch, Somerset was ordering and organising it. Nor did Canteloupe object; for Somerset knew a lot about food and somehow hypnotised waiters into absolute compliance, like a snake.

'The Director of Features says,' Somerset intoned, 'that while there are no specific provisions in Tom's contract as to moral respectability, there is a clause which requires that he should be resident in the United Kingdom during the period of his appointment and that he should retain "the necessary capacity to fulfil his obligations to the Corporation". Obviously, if Tom went mad or broke his neck the BBC would be entitled to terminate the agreement.'

'So where does this Maisie come in? Is she going to drive

him potty or break his neck with a poker?'

'Maisie,' said Somerset, 'is a whore. A very accomplished whore.'

'Lead me to her.'

'I'll certainly give you an introduction, but that must come later. The point, here and now, is that Maisie of all people is qualified to make such a disastrous fool out of Tom that the BBC would have no alternative but to declare him thenceforth unfit "to fulfil his obligations".'

'Tom Llewyllyn,' said Canteloupe, 'is not an easy man to make a fool of.'

'Tom Llewyllyn,' said Somerset, 'used to be very, very partial to whores. In fact, Canteloupe, whores were all that he was partial to—though God knows he had enough opportunities elsewhere.'

'You mean ... he liked paying for it?'

'I mean he only liked it when he was paying for it.'

'But since he's been married?'

Somerset shrugged.

'He'll have *missed* paying for it.'

'However much he's missed it, that's no reason why he should let this baggage make a fool of him. Not to the extent that you seem to count on.'

'You don't know Maisie,' Somerset said. 'She really is rather special. She's nothing much to look at, you understand, but she has a genius for her work.'

While Somerset Lloyd-James was lunching with Lord Canteloupe, Tom Llewyllyn was lunching down in Cambridge, with Robert Reculver Constable, the Provost of Lancaster College.

'The programmes,' Tom explained, 'will be monthly. We are starting at the end of May with an analysis, conducted by Hugh Trevor-Roper, of resurgent Nazism in Western Germany.'

'Very salutary,' said Constable. 'It's high time *that* cat was let properly out of the bag.'

'I hope to let out a lot of cats—even fiercer ones,' Tom said. 'I am particularly keen to emphasise the random nature of historical events. To show that we have very little control over anything that happens and that even when we think we know what we are doing we are usually doing something quite different.'

'Hmm,' grunted Constable, who was a good socialist and believed very firmly in planning. 'Concrete instance, please.'

'Cyprus,' said Tom. 'We thought we were dealing with a spontaneous demand for self-determination. In fact, however, the Cypriots were being unconsciously pressured into demanding something which they didn't want and then into using means they detested to get it. We weren't quarrelling with the Cypriots at all, really, we were fighting an American secret service conspiracy to humiliate and dispossess us. A perfect example of history making fools out of us all, since neither of the apparent protagonists—Britain and Cyprus—had the slightest control over anything that happened.'

'But not exactly a random affair, even on your theory. At least the Americans knew what they were doing.'

'Very few of them knew about it at all. And the only motive of those that did was atavistic jealousy of the British.'

'Still not entirely random.'

'Not far off it. There was no policy, only whim.'

'Very well,' Constable said; 'and what evidence can you produce?'

Tom outlined what he hoped to be able to prove.

'If all goes well,' he concluded, 'I want to make this the subject of our programme at the end of June.'

'And why are you telling me about it?'

'Gray himself,' said Tom, 'is too badly disfigured to appear on television. He will probably speak the narrative, which he himself will write, over the film sequences which we shall construct to illustrate it, but he cannot address the audience in person. In any case, I need someone more authoritative to do that: someone of prestige and known impartiality, who will summarise and endorse the proofs presented. In one word, Provost Constable, I need you.'

'I'm an economist, not an historian.'

'You are a figure,' said Tom, 'of the utmost academic repute. You are known as a man who will accept nothing without flawless evidence. That is what I need.'

'That's as may be,' said Constable, flattered despite himself: 'but what makes you think that Gray's evidence will be flawless?'

'I can't guarantee that, of course. But if I give you immediate access to it when Gray returns, will you agree to assess it?'

'I don't see why not.'

'And if you find it sound, will you appear on the programme and say so?'

'I don't much care for arc lamps and glamour.'

'I wouldn't want you if you did. I want you to be bleak,
even boring, and totally undramatic. I want you to sum up
as precisely and as prosaically as the most scrupulous judge
in the kingdom.'

Constable rapped his coffee spoon on the table. First a
few isolated beats, then a swift and continuous tattoo.

'I may write my own summary?' he asked.

'Of course.'

'And I may examine the film sequences you propose to
use to make sure that these do not distort fact or give rise to
false emphasis?'

'Certainly. When they are ready.'

'Very well,' said Constable, 'I'll do it. But if I were you, I
shouldn't rely too much on this man Gray. Years ago,
when I was tutor here, I had to refuse him admission to this
college.'

'So I've heard.'

'But did you hear why? It was because he was found to
have deceived. To have deceived and betrayed people who
loved him for the sake of his own squalid pleasure.'

'I think you'll find that he's changed, Provost. Besides,'
Tom said, 'if he tries to deceive us, no one will be quicker to
find him out than you.'

'He very nearly wasn't found out before,' said Constable.
'He might never have been if he hadn't lost his head. First
he deceived, and then, at a critical moment, he gave himself
away because he lost his head. Unreliable either way, you
see.'

'I think you're being rather hard, Provost. Years ago,
when he was very young, Fielding Gray was pitiably exposed and then fully punished for all that he had done.
Why not leave it at that?'

'I'll be glad to,' said Constable; 'but can *he* leave it at
that?'

As soon as he arrived in Athens, Fielding had sat himself
down in the Grande Bretagne Hotel and written to General
Grivas in the terms already rehearsed with Leonard Perci-

val. His experience of some years back, he wrote, while he was fighting against EOKA in Cyprus, had given him an immense respect for the General personally, and an abiding interest in the General's military techniques. However, since he had been engaged by the BBC to investigate Cypriot affairs, certain people (he was not entirely sure who they were) seemed to have misconceived his motives as hostile to the present interests of Cyprus and to the good name of those who had taken part in her liberation. If the General would grant him the privilege of an interview, he would undertake to remove these misapprehensions; and having done so, he would be greatly honoured if the General would condescend to answer certain questions about the strategies and conceptions involved in the Cyprus campaign. The information would be used to prepare a responsible television programme, and it was also hoped to produce a detailed study in the form of a book by the writer of the present letter ... who was, my dear General, yours sincerely Fielding Gray, sometime Major and Officer Commanding the 10th Sabre Squadron of the 49th Earl Hamilton's Light Dragoons (Cyprus 1956–8).

The next day, Fielding made an expedition by taxi to Delphi and did not return until late in the evening. Since he had been feeling more and more doubtful as the day went on about the reply (if any) which his letter to Grivas would elicit, he was surprised to find that an envelope had been delivered by messenger that afternoon and that it contained a very courteous note written (like Fielding's) in literary Greek. The General regretted that he must be absent from Athens for the next seven days, but would be delighted to entertain Major Gray to luncheon at one o'clock on the afternoon following his return. The General was conscious of the honour of receiving an officer from so distinguished a regiment as Earl Hamilton's Light Dragoons, whose bearing and dexterity he had much admired.

So that's it, Fielding thought. Nothing to do now but wait. He composed a brief despatch to Leonard Percival, c/o The American Express, Roma, and another to Tom at the BBC; then he settled down to prepare an elaborate schedule of sight-seeing and related reading to fill in the next week.

Angela Tuck, having finished Fielding's novels, had nothing

much to do with herself, and was therefore not at all pleased when Max rang up the next morning to say that he must now spend a third day and a third night away in Famagusta, where he had found a building suitable to house a casino and also several allies who were well placed to help him obtain the good will of the Administration.

After receiving this telephone call, Angela fretted and fiddled the morning away, ate a large English-style lunch, slept through the afternoon, awoke cross and sour-mouthed at six o'clock, and contrived to spend the next two hours bathing and dressing. During these two hours she drank several large whiskies, and by the time she had put down a pint of red wine with what little she could swallow of her English-style dinner and then poured two neat brandies on top of the whole mixture, she was positively twitching for action. Max, she remembered, had spoken of a wine-shop called Clito's, where the drink was supposed to be good and the company various; so thither, having with some difficulty obtained directions from a disapproving hall porter, she took her crepuscular way.

Some years before, Clito's shop had been only a dank cave filled with barrels and his clientele largely masculine and indigenous. However, the praise which several bibulous men of letters had bestowed on his wines and his tolerance had made Clito famous and enabled him to move into more commodious premises, in which he was now (to the fury of the men of letters) operating as a considerable tourist attraction, with prices to match. The arrival of an unaccompanied female, which in the era of the dank cave would have caused grave displeasure, was nothing out of the way these days; and though survivors of the original clientele frowned into their glasses, a new and younger class of Cypriot customer perked up, looked knowing, and dragged on its trouser legs to reveal large sections of bare calf, which were then laid out on available chairs for Angela's inspection.

There was only one firm rule of the house—that no native might make a direct approach to a foreigner or overtly solicit a drink. Smiles and displays of calf were as far as the young jackals of Kyrenia might go, and to these Angela remained indifferent. Or so it seemed. In fact, she was quietly employing a calculus of her own from which, having first made rough appraisals of shoulders, biceps and hips, she was able to arrive at a computation of the probable priapic capacities of all present. Only when she had done this, and added in certain other factors, such as facial appeal, skin textures and colouring, would she arrive at her final selection; and being a woman of great experience, she took her time. Meanwhile, she tried a bottle of Cypriot rosé, changed to a coarse local brandy and soda, changed again to a more refined local brandy without soda, reflected that she was too old to risk inferior liquor, and grievously offended Clito, who retained a fierce pride in the vines of his island, by making him bring out the bottle of Remy Martin which he reluctantly kept in reserve for faddy drinkers.

After about three-quarters of an hour, Angela decided on a boy with thin, hairy legs and smooth, pretty face. The contrast between the effeminacy above and the hirsute exhibition below titillated the perverse streak in her and also promised, when she consulted her mental records of this type, a graceful and not ungenerous sexual physique. So she called for another glass, raised the bottle of Remy Martin, waggled it like a pendulum, and beckoned to the goat-legged youth.

The youth rose, snorting and libidinous. Hardly had he reached her table, however, when a tall and bland-faced man, dressed in a beautiful suit of fawn gaberdine, took him by the shoulder, turned him smartly round, and pushed him back towards his friends. The boy turned at the man with a swift and saurian flick of the head, but as soon as he could see the interloper properly he nodded gravely and withdrew. The man sat down at Angela's table without speaking, waved at Clito, who was already bringing him a carafe of white wine, and then smiled at Angela, who had been about to issue a shrill protest, in a way that somehow seemed to offer untold riches in this world or even the next, to offer the Forbidden City, at the least, or the Golden Apples of the Sun.

'Mrs Tuck?' said the man.

What a come-down after that smile, she thought: a smile such as a jinn out of the lamp might give to a princess of Araby—and then the two words as bare and flat as floorboards.

'Mrs Tuck,' she said. 'And you?'

Clito poured the stranger some white wine from the

carafe and then, giving Angela a look in which distaste was now mingled with new respect, filled her glass with Remy Martin from the bottle on the table. Plainly, she thought, this man is someone; merely by sitting at my table he has raised my status.

'What do you want?' she said briskly. 'And what do I call you?'

'Earle ... with an *e*.'

'Well, Mr Earle——'

'—Just Earle. I must apologise,' he said in an American accent which was all but entirely anglicised, 'for changing your plans for the evening. But I don't think you'll regret it.'

Again the smile, promising undreamed of pleasures and enchanted islands in which to enjoy them. A pure con, thought Angela, and nerved herself to resist.

'You haven't changed anything yet,' she said. 'You've merely interfered and delayed.'

'If you offered those boys a hundred pounds,' he said, 'not one of them would come near you now without my permission.'

'Bloody conceit,' Angela said.

She beckoned once more to the pretty face with the goat-legs. The boy stared straight back over her head and didn't move a muscle.

'You see?'

'Then I'll make do with my own company.' She turned to Clito, who was hovering behind his counter. 'My bill, please,' she said.

Clito shrugged, shook his head, and spread his arms wide.

'He won't take your money.'

'Then he can go without it.'

Angela rose, walked steadily to the door and out into the empty street. As she went, the stranger said something in conversational tones and demotic Greek. There was a scurrying and a clattering behind her, and within five seconds she found that she was surrounded by the boys and youths from inside. They did not impede her; they merely formed a circle round her and walked along at the same pace as she did. Then the stranger, Earle, was beside her.

'We'll go to the harbour,' he said, and took her arm.

The circular cortege turned down a side street, and then

down another. From this it emerged on to a short quay, the far end of which sloped down, like a ramp, on to a beach of shingle.

'Where are you taking me?'

'A little al fresco celebration, Mrs Tuck. Believe me, you'll enjoy it.'

They tramped across the shingle, away from the sea. Somewhere up on Angela's left the fort was hanging in the darkness, while ahead was a mass of large rocks. One of the boys led the way to a gap between two of these; Earle followed him through the gap, gently pulling Angela along behind him; and the rest of the boys, some eight or nine of them, came in single file after Angela. The gap led into a rather wider passage, so that now she was able to come up with Earle and walk by his side.

'Intriguing, isn't it?' he said.

The boy in front led on for perhaps twenty yards, after which the passage narrowed once more and then immediately widened again to turn itself into an egg-shaped arena, closed off at the far end, of fifteen yards in length by some six or seven where the oval was widest.

'Nothing to be frightened of,' said Earle in a soothing voice.

'I'm not frightened.'

Nor was she. For one thing, she had had a great deal to drink, and for another she was now pretty certain what was in train. Here was a rich American who was paying these boys to mount some sort of spectacle. For whatever reason, her own presence, or participation, was going to give him an additional thrill. So be it. If only he had come out with his proposition straight away in Clito's, instead of annoying her by putting on such a silly and pretentious act, Angela would have agreed to join in from the word go and would even have offered to share expenses. She liked a daisy chain from time to time, and the American himself, if too conventionally cut altogether to suit her tastes, was undeniably appetising. By and large, then, she was fully prepared to assist in anything which might be toward, and she looked with pleasure round the little grotto which had been selected. Her only regrets were that the floor was still of shingle, not sand, and that it would be too dark to appreciate the nuances of the entertainment.

Of this, it now appeared, she herself was to be the centre.

All at once the boys from Clito's closed in on her. She just had time to notice that Earle himself had backed away against the rock before she was lifted by a dozen hands and laid gently on the ground. The dozen hands now started to caress her in a dozen different ways, while out of the dark the pretty face she had fancied in the wine-shop loomed down from one side to kiss her on eyes, ears and lips. As the face hovered and dipped at her own, hovered and dipped again, always close enough to blot out what little she might actually have seen in the darkness, it began to seem to her as though it were this one boy alone who was making love to her but this one boy somehow endowed with so many limbs and so much skill that he could rouse pleasure simultaneously in every place of her body. Instead of being fumbled by a crowd, she was being gloriously embraced by an immortal god with a face like Cupid's and the magical ability to make one mouth do the work of ten, ten fingers do the work of a hundred. From head to foot, every nerve in her which was apt for stimulation was being stimulated; she was, literally, one mass of desire. As the tongues and fingers went on busily about their tasks, she felt her damp thighs being slowly prised apart, The god was poised, he was about to enter.

Then she was lying alone on the cold shingle, with only the disarray of her clothes to prove that she had not imagined the entire scene.

'Come back,' she called; 'come back.'

'I told you you wouldn't regret it,' said Earle, who was now standing above her. 'An amusing idea, which originated with the Empress Theodora in her younger and jollier days.'

'Bring them back.'

'All right.'

There was a quick flurry in the darkness and once again her god was loving her tenfold.

'What can you tell me about Fielding Gray?' said Earle.

'What's Fielding Gray to you?' she mumbled, while the pretty Cupid face brushed lightly over her cheeks.

'Tell me about him.'

'Nothing to tell.'

The god stopped loving.

'They're bored with your old body,' said Earle. 'You must excite them. Tell them what you did with Fielding Gray.'

Angela started to tell. Slowly the god moved into action again, leaving her lips free to utter the phrases which roused his divine lust.

'I see,' said Earle at length. 'This boy the two of you talked about ... this boy that killed himself. Describe him.'

Once again Angela's thighs were parted and the god was poised.

'I never saw him.'

The god perceptibly withdrew.

'Christ, Christ,' she screamed; 'don't let him go away from me.'

'Excite him then. Tell him about this boy. He likes hearing about boys.'

Yes, thought Angela wildly, all gods are bisexual.

'I can show you a book,' she babbled, 'Fielding wrote a book. Fair-haired ... strong limbs but delicate too ... light silver hairs on his legs...'

'Go on.'

She felt the poised god move very slightly nearer.

'I don't know. Yes, I do. There's a statue like him. Fielding told me. In some porch or something the Americans made in Athens, a statue of a boy with a flute.'

'How very convenient,' said Earle.

He snapped his fingers, and the god sank his sacred flesh slowly into Angela's, working the while at her whole body with his tongues and his fingers and his other immortal members.

'No,' said Maisie; 'I won't do it.'

'Didn't you hear properly?' said Somerset Lloyd-James. 'Five hundred pounds, I said. To say nothing of an introduction to a new and noble client.'

'New and noble clients are all right,' said Maisie, 'if they still want to come. But I won't do what you ask to this Tom Thingamabob at the BBC.'

'All you've got to do is to meet him, get him started ... you know ... and then go there and kick up a thcene.'

Somerset still tended to revert to his childhood lisp when he was excited or upset.

'I don't go out to work. I do it here. What you're asking,' said Maisie, 'isn't decent. It isn't fair and it isn't professional.'

'Now, look here, Maithie——'

'—And you look here,' she said. 'I'm paid to make men come. I don't mind which way I do it—as you very well know by now—because that's what they're paying me for, and as jobs go in this world it's as fair and as square as most others I've heard of. But what you're asking's different. You're asking me to make a fool of someone who's never done me any harm and who's got his job to do the same as I've got mine. If a man wants to knock on my door and says, "Maisie, here's a tenner, make me come", then I'll do my best for him and welcome. But if a man wants nothing to do with me, I want nothing to do with him, and I'm not going out anywhere for the sake of stirring up trouble.'

'I dare say we could go a hundred higher.'

'Court cases,' said Maisie, 'names in the papers. I'd never have any peace and quiet again. So either get out of here, Mister Somerset Lloyd-James, MP, or tell me what I *can* do for you. Who do you want me to be this week? Your governess? Or the chamber-maid at that hotel by the sea-side? Or that jolly Aunt who played hot cockles with you in the back of her Rolls on the way back from the circus? We haven't had *her* for nearly a year now.'

'None of those, I think,' said Somerset, still lisping. 'Can we have the woman on the train? You know ... when there ithn't a corridor and she's thuddenly taken thort?'

Captain Detterling went to dinner in Chelsea with Gregory and Isobel Stern. Although Gregory had finally agreed to do the Cavafy memoirs, he was still proving obstinate in other matters and relations at the office were rather strained. However, it was understood that this dinner was a social occasion, and since Detterling was far too well mannered to talk business when he was not supposed to, all would have been well had not Gregory himself raised the topic.

'Today,' he said, 'I signed a contract for a book which propounds a new theory of the Crucifixion.'

'What new theory?' Detterling asked.

'That the Romans were exclusively responsible.'

'But we had all that,' said Detterling, 'ten years ago. Late in 1951, the Jewish historian Shalom Franklyn published an exceedingly long and detailed book about it. It's all been said, Gregory.'

'Then it should be said again. Because people have

already forgotten.'

'They have not forgotten,' said Detterling. 'On the contrary, they remember very clearly that Franklyn was shown to be wrong. He succeeded in shifting a bit more of the guilt on to the Romans, and he blew up the notion that Pilate was a humane and civilised man; but he didn't prove, because he couldn't, that the Jews were spotless in the affair.'

'This new book I have bought does that.'

'Then its author is either unscholarly or deluded.'

'Why are you so keen that the Jews should have killed Jesus Christ?'

'I'm not *blaming* them, Gregory. Christ asked for everything he got. I'm just saying that this particular controversy is dead.'

'And if there were new documents?'

'Are there?'

'Professor Bamberger, the author, claims to have inspected——'

'—*Claims to have inspected*. What's the matter with you, Gregory?'

'So Bamberger is a liar?' said Gregory, thumping the table. 'He is a Jew and therefore a liar? So that is it?'

'Boys, boys,' said Isobel. 'You don't want me to miscarry? Let's talk about something nice.'

'So talking about Jews is not nice?'

'For Christ's sake shut up,' Isobel said. 'Has anyone heard anything more about Fielding in Greece?'

'You should know. It is you that is always dreaming of him.'

'Not for a long time,' said Isobel. 'I used to think there was something psychic between Fielding and me, but since the baby's been coming it's all stopped.'

'Nature,' said Detterling: 'I'm told she protects pregnant women against any form of worry by releasing a special secretion into the blood. Your body manufactures its own opiate.'

'Yes,' said Gregory. 'Nature would not wish you to worry about Fielding at a time like this.'

'I never worried. I just had hunches about what was happening to him. Or what was going to.'

'I must say,' said Detterling, 'I should very much like to know.'

'One morning,' said Gregory, 'he will wake up in Athens

and say to himself. "My God, how could I be such a fool?"
Then he will come back to us and start writing novels again.
Love's Jest Book,' he said to Detterling, 'is still selling
slowly but steadily.'

Isobel shuddered.

'I hated that book,' she said.

'May one ask why?'

'There's a light, bright flicker of madness in it. Any sane
man would have forgotten all that stuff years ago.'

'No writer is strictly sane. Nor are people who have
psychic hunches.'

'Well, pregnancy seems to have stopped my kind of madness,' said Isobel. 'What can we do for Fielding's?'

'Make as much money out of it for him as we can,'
Detterling said. 'Then when he finally goes raving at least
he'll be able to afford a comfortable bin.'

Earle Restarick flew from Nicosia to Athens. The minute
he arrived, he took a taxi to the Agora and went straight to
the reconstructed Stoa at the far end of it. He walked along
this until he came to the boy with the flute, examined the
statue with great care, and then knocked on the door beside
it. When the door had been unlocked from within, he
passed into a small and windowless room which contained
several metal filing cabinets, a desk with one chair, and a lot
of broken statuary.

'How's the ancient world?' he said to the man who had
admitted him—a thin, short man, with a nose as long as a
hockey stick and a sensitive mouth.

'Preferable to the modern one. How's the Great Game?'

'There is an interesting problem to, hand. Does the
American School of Greek Studies in Athens run to a
knowledge of comparative ethnology?'

'Try us.'

'That statue just outside in the portico?'

'A copy from a late Hellenistic original. Probably made
about AD 100. What's that got to do with ethnology?'

'Comparative ethnology. The Grecian type seems to have
changed since the late Hellenistic period.'

'There have been a lot of mixed marriages round here in
the last 2,000 years.'

'There must be some areas—remote areas—when you can
still find the classic article.'

'Only flukes, accidental throwbacks. For 2,000 years the whole of Greece has been swarming with Syrians, Romans, Franks, Lombards, Venetians, Egyptians and Turks. No area is remote enough to have escaped the attentions of that little lot. If you want the classical Greek type, there's only one hope for you.'

'Oh?'

'Find a German got from the time of the occupation. There are a few about. Blond, blue-eyed, straight-limbed—a very passable imitation of the old Dorian strain. The only people in this country who still look like real Greeks,' said the man with the hockey-stick nose, 'were fathered in the forties by the Hun.'

'And so,' said Somerset Lloyd-James to Lord Canteloupe, 'there's nothing doing with Maisie. Though she'll be glad to see you personally in her professional capacity.'

He handed Canteloupe a slip of paper on which a telephone number was written.

'But,' Somerset went on, 'as regards Tom Llewyllyn there is another possibility.'

Canteloupe sighed.

'Here we go again,' he said.

'On the contrary, we don't go anywhere. This time we just sit absolutely still,' said Somerset, 'holding our breath and waiting for it.'

'Waiting for what?'

'Nemesis,' said Somerset with relish.

'Do you have to talk like a schoolmaster?'

'Nemesis,' Somerset pursued, 'which in this case will come, not as the scourge of pride, but as the scourge of innocence. It really is exquisitely funny.'

He started to chortle, sounding like something behind the wainscot in a story by Edgar Allan Poe.

'If you don't stop that horrible row,' said the Marquis Canteloupe, 'and tell me what you're talking about, I shall hit you on your bald, yellow head.'

Honking and wheezing with his macabre merriment, Somerset began to tell him.

Three days before he was due to see General Grivas, Fielding's sight-seeing schedule took him once more to Delphi, where he proposed to spend the night and make a more detailed exploration than he had had time for on his previous visit. He left Athens in a hired car (self-drive) at ten in the morning, stopped on the way at Thebes to look at the museum, and arrived at Delphi in time for a late lunch. Having then established himself in the Xenia, in a room which looked straight out over the gorge, he drove along the hillside to the ancient site and began his carefully planned tour of inspection.

After fussing about for some time among the 'treasuries' in the temple enclosure, he sat down on a stone and read Pausanias' account (in the Loeb edition, which he had procured from the bookshop off Constitution Square) of the shrine and its environs. He then walked on up to the temple itself, peered down into the chasm from which the priestess had uttered the oracles, and started on a conscientious examination of the inner precinct. It was while he was doing this, and cursing himself, not for the first time, for his contemptible knowledge of archaeology, that he began to feel he was being watched.

At first the feeling was in no way uncomfortable; it was rather as though some tutelary spirit of the place, not the god himself but some otherwise unoccupied minor deputy, was courteously hovering nearby in case he should require direction or assistance. It was, he told himself, a compliment to the interest he was taking; he was being recognised as a worthwhile guest. As time went on, however, and the feeling that he was observed grew steadily more insistent, he began to wish that his companion (for as such he now regarded him) would find some means of declaring himself. Repeatedly he looked about him, hoping that the undeniable presence might take bodily form, but the only bodies visible were those of two crestfallen Americans and their voluble guide, who was issuing an interminable harangue, down by the treasuries, about the Amphictyonic Council.

Anxious to get out of range of the guide's clacking monologue, Fielding now left the temple and took the path up through the trees towards the theatre. The guardian presence went with him. Somewhere in the pine-trees, he could not be sure on which side of the path, an intelligence which wished to communicate with his own was lurking along beside him. An intelligence? Say rather a fancy, a dream, a vision: something, in any case, which wanted to draw nearer to him but which, as he now realised, could not declare itself further unless he himself were to perform some act of prayer or ritual, utter some word or think some thought, which would give the spirit shape and enable it to come to him.

What prayer? What word? What thought?

'Who are you?' he called. 'What do you want?'

The presence lingered but came no nearer. Slowly he walked on up the path. He knew now that he needed more than mere words to speak; he needed to imagine something, or to remember something, or to feel something. A wish or an emotion? What? For if he could only make the mental effort required of him, he would be proved worthy and granted the vision. If not ... well, it would linger awhile as it was now, but before long it would go sadly away, betrayed by his own failure of spirit. He must prove himself before it departed. What did it want of him?

He emerged from among the trees and found himself standing at the top of the theatre, looking down the stone tiers on to the stage below, and then beyond it, to the gorge above which the eagles slowly circled, to the bare, black ridge on the other side, and then away to the west, where the sun was sinking above the Gulf of Corinth. As he watched the eagles gliding, and as he saw the sea come glittering and creeping up to the olive coast below, he realised, for the first time in his life and with a physical pang which stirred in his body like lust, what it meant to be in a sacred place. He sat down on the stone ledge at the top of the theatre and burst into tears.

For some time he kept his head lowered, while the tears dripped off his face and on to his feet. When he began to recover himself, he took a handkerchief from his pocket and put it up towards his eye. As he did so, he heard a voice which whispered into his ear the one word:

'Please.'

He looked to his left and his right; he looked behind him; nobody.

'Please,' the voice whispered, 'please. Don't cry. Please.'

My tears have let the presence speak to me, he thought. What more must I do to see it?

'Please. I am here. Please.'

He raised his head again and this time looked down on to the stage. In the middle of it was a figure. A boy. Of course, he thought: in this theatre of all theatres the lightest sigh from the stage, the fall of a rose leaf, can be heard in every part.

'I am here. Please.'

Fielding started to walk down the steps to the stage. As he drew nearer to the figure below, he saw that the boy's short fair hair curled above a square, creamy forehead; as he came nearer still, he saw that the eyes were mild and wide-set, that the nose was soft, that the lips were full and curved slightly downwards, and that there was a cleft in the chin. Dear God, he thought, he's been given back to me; that's what was promised in the pine-trees; for the price of my tears he's been given back to me.

'Christopher, oh Christopher,' he called, 'is it really you?'

The boy did not answer, but held out both arms and raised his mouth for a kiss.

Maisie rang up Tom Llewyllyn at the BBC.

'You don't know me,' she said, 'but I want to see you. I want to give you a warning.'

'I'm afraid I don't quite understand.'

'No, of course you don't, and I can't tell you more on the 'phone. Come round to my place at six this evening, and I'll tell you what I can.'

'I don't think I can do that.'

'Look,' said Maisie. 'You don't know me and I don't know you, but I know who you are and I know some of your friends. Fielding Gray for one—he's told me quite a lot about you. But it's not him I want to talk about, it's other so-called friends who are getting ready to land you in the dirt. So if you know what's good for you, you'll clean out your ears ready to listen and come round here this evening at six.'

Then Maisie told him where to come and rang off.

In the room which looked out over the gorge, Fielding looked down on the firm, brown stomach and lowered his

face to kiss it, while the boy moved his hands in his hair.
Naked, the boy was just as Fielding had always remembered
him. But there were differences in other things. There was
no shyness, now that he had come back after all these years,
and no shame. Instead there was pride of flesh and com-
plicity in desire.

'Christopher,' murmured Fielding into the brown skin,
'where have you been?'

'My name is Nicos.'

'Now it is. But I shall still call you Christopher. Do you
mind?'

'It can make no difference.' The boy went on playing with
Fielding's hair. 'What happened to your face?'

'I was hurt in an explosion. Does it ... upset you?'

'It can make no difference,' the boy said again, and ran
one finger down to the base of Fielding's spine.

'So you see,' Maisie said to Tom, 'Somerset Lloyd-James is
trying to do you down.'

'But you've refused to help him, you say.'

'He'll find someone else ... or some other way.'

'Fore-warned is fore-armed.'

'That's what I thought.'

'Thank you,' said Tom. 'Why did you bother?'

'Because I didn't like the smell of it. And then, you're a
friend of Fielding's.'

'Are you fond of Fielding?'

'I've known him a long time.'

'I see ... I'll tell you something,' Tom said. 'Somerset
was right. If you'd set yourself out to do what he asked, it
could have worked. I'm married, and I love my wife, but it
could still have worked.'

'Should I be flattered?' asked Maisie.

'No. It's not you, attractive as you are. It's the set-up. It's
... forgive me ... It's the brevity, the lewdness, the disgust.
That's what I always went for.'

'I understand,' said Maisie placidly.

Tom looked at her, panting slightly. His hand went towards his breast pocket, but then he closed his eyes, shook
his head, turned firmly about and walked from Maisie's
flat.

'I'm due in Athens in a day or two,' said Fielding. He got

off the bed, went to the window and looked out over the darkening gorge. 'But once I've finished my business there, we can go anywhere we like.'

'I'll go wherever you wish,' the boy said, 'but not to Athens.'

'It won't be for long.'

'Not to Athens.'

'But why on earth not?'

'*Not to Athens.*'

The police, thought Fielding. Some trouble like that. Christopher was in trouble with the police, he thought, seventeen years ago.

'Then I must go alone. You can wait for me wherever you choose, and I'll join you as soon as I can.'

'If you leave me,' the boy said, 'I shan't be able to wait for you. Anywhere.'

'I don't understand.'

'You've been very fortunate to find me—to find me once more, as you say. If you let me go ... a second time ... I shall have gone for ever.'

'But why? *Why?...*'

'Because I shall have been ... recalled.'

Like Eurydice, Fielding thought, sweating with fear.

'Come here,' the boy said, 'come to the bed.'

As Fielding went towards the bed, the boy held out his arms as he had on the theatre stage that afternoon. He kissed the shiny pink skin, then took Fielding's head between his hands, cradled it in his warm belly, and stroked Fielding's hair.

'You must not leave me,' the boy said; 'you must not let me go again.'

'Why are you home so late?' said Patricia to Tom in Southwell Gardens.

'Because I've been with a whore.'

As Patricia slowly opened her mouth, a wail like that of a siren rose from somewhere down in her stomach and came spiralling out with steadily increasing volume. Baby, not to be left out of the act, emitted shrill screams of accusation at short intervals of deadly regularity.

'It wasn't what you think,' said Tom.

He picked up the howling Baby, thrust her out into the little passage, then closed and locked the living-room door.

'It wasn't what you think,' he repeated to Patricia, 'but it might very easily have been. Because there's a hot, dirty, ratty side to me which I've never shown you yet but which has only been waiting to come out.'

Patricia looked at him, silent now.

'I might have taken it out on that whore,' Tom said, 'and kept it from you that much longer. But I think it's time you knew about it, once and for all.'

He forced her down on the sofa.

'For better or for worse.'

He fumbled with her clothes and his own.

'Quick,' he said, 'hot, nasty and quick.'

'Tom ... *Tom*.'

'Into the bushes,' Tom hissed, 'and do it before anyone comes. Standing up or like the dogs. Dirt. Sweat. Stink. Quick, Patricia, quick.'

'Oh God,' she whimpered, as Baby hammered on the door. 'Oh dear God,' she panted, 'it's never been like this. Quick, Tom, quick. Like the dogs, Tom. QUICK.'

I've got to go through with it, Fielding thought. I've got to see Grivas and get that evidence for Tom.

He looked at the sleeping boy beside him. The fair hair was plastered with sweat over the temples and the brow; the full lips pouted, as if ready to be wakened by a kiss.

No. Think. I've taken on a job, for which I'm being very well paid. Succeed in this, and it could mean more jobs, more money, later on. Fame. Anyway, Tom is relying on me, trusting me to do this for him.

But I could always say I'd been with Grivas and failed. (Those lips.) After all, I've been through a lot already, what right have they to force me into more?

But Tom didn't force me. He asked me if I wanted to go on with it, and I said yes.

Those lips, those cheeks.

But leave Tom aside, and to hell with the BBC, the job is one that ought to be, that must be done. I want to do it. I want to finish what I've started, now that I'm so near. I want to destroy Restarick, show up the whole rotten business, warn everybody what goes on.

But if I go to Athens, I shall lose him. For the second time.

Slowly, Fielding drew down the sheet. Chest. Belly.

Loins. Thighs. Soft skin, silver down, catching the early morning light. The boy whimpered slightly in his sleep, and Fielding settled the sheet back over him, shuddering with joy at the sight he had just seen.

If I go to Athens, I shall lose it all.

I must go to Athens. For my career, for Tom's friendship, for truth.

But I am not due in Athens until one p.m. of the day after tomorrow. Two more days, two more nights.

'Take care,' said Patricia to Tom at breakfast.

'Take care?'

'You know ... What you told me last night. What that woman——'

'——Maisie——'

'——What Maisie was warning you about.'

Baby, who sensed peace and solidarity, gurgled happily.

'I'm grateful to Maisie,' said Patricia, 'for making it so much better for us.'

'It was all right before.'

'Not like that, though, never like that. And I'm grateful to her for warning you. You must take care, Tom. Why do they want to harm you?'

'I'm not sure. I think ... that they think ... that I may be going to broadcast something that will make trouble for them. There have been hints from other quarters.'

'Must you go on with it?'

Tom shrugged.

'Yes,' he said. 'But if I keep my nose clean, there's nothing they can do.'

Patricia kissed him gaily on the lips.

'Then keep your nose clean,' she said.

Fielding and Nicos went for a walk along the shore of the Corinthian Gulf, between Itea and Galaxheidhi. For much of the way the olive trees came crowding down almost to the sea, leaving only a thin strand of beach. Since the afternoon was very hot, they walked mostly in the shade of the olive trees.

'Why do you not ask me,' said Nicos, 'who I am, where I come from? Such questions should be asked between friends.'

'I'm not sure that I want to know the answers.'

'Then I shall ask you. Who are you, Fielding Gray? Where do you come from?'

'I am a writer of books, and I come from England.'

'And you have business in Athens. You will not go there now, I think.'

'I must go.'

Nicos pursed his lips and moved on ahead, kicking at the ground with every third or fourth step.

'But not yet,' said Fielding as he caught up with him.

'When?'

'Need we talk of it?'

'Yes. I wish to know.'

'In two days' time.'

'You must not go. Please. You must not leave Nicos. You must not leave ... Christopher.'

He pronounced the name as if it had been Christopheros without the final syllable: Christopher.

'Why cannot you wait for me while I go?'

'I shall swim now,' Nicos said.

'Take care.'

'I am a good swimmer.'

Nicos stripped down to his underpants, while Fielding settled himself on the ground, supporting his back against an olive trunk. From where he sat he had a clear view of the sea, and of Nicos as he bobbed and duck-dived some thirty yards out. Who is he? Fielding thought: where does he come from? But as he had told Nicos a few minutes before, he did not really want to know. It could make no difference. For on the one hand, Nicos was just a little pick-up, who had been waiting for a tourist, any tourist, and nobody wanted to know who pick-ups were and where they came from: while on the other hand, he was the gift promised by some god in a sacred precinct, and of such it was forbidden to enquire the origin. Enough, either way, that he was Christopher come back again, just as if Christopher had been reborn, when he died nearly seventeen years ago, and had grown up as Nicos, in a different land. Nicos' age was right for that, Fielding thought. He was slightly under seventeen, to all appearance, and could well have been born during that summer of 1945, when Christopher had been betrayed and died. Would Nicos die too if he were betrayed ... if Fielding went to Athens? But why should this be betrayal?

Fielding's head sunk forward on his chest. Eurydice, he thought. When she was taken for the second time (*ceu fumus in auras*, like smoke into the air, into thin air), Orpheus was forbidden ever to seek her out again. *Nec portitor Orci Amplius objectam passus transire paludem;* nor did the gatekeeper of hell suffer him any more to pass the barrier of the marsh. Eurydice, beyond the marsh in hell; Christopher, Nicos, beyond the marsh in hell. Or so he might be if Fielding left him to go to Athens. Like many that had been so beautiful. *Tot milia formosarum ... formosorum ...*

When he awoke there was no sign of Nicos in the sea.

'Christopher,' he called at once; then 'Nicos ... Nicos.'

Ceu fumus in auras.

'Nicos ... *Nicos.*'

He rose to his feet and ran across the beach. But his legs had been infected with his panic and would not carry him; he sprawled full length and lay shaking and desperate, until a wave licked at his face. Then he raised himself on one elbow.

'NICOS,' he screamed.

'Here I am.'

There, at the edge of the olive grove. Quite naked now, legs crossed, leaning against a tree-trunk.

'I thought ... I thought ...'

'I was drying myself in the sun. You ran straight past me ... lying on the beach. I am sorry if you are upset.'

'I'm all right, now. Oh, Nicos.'

'Why do you look at me like that?'

'You know why.'

Nicos grinned and flaunted himself.

'Come here,' he said: 'Then you can look as close as you please.'

Tom Llewyllyn rang up Provost Constable at Lancaster College.

'I've just had a letter from Gray,' Tom said; 'he is to have an interview with Grivas in two days' time from now.'

'As to that,' said Constable, 'we shall see what we shall see. But there's something else I want to talk to you about. Can you spare a few minutes?'

'Why not? The BBC's paying for the call.'

'Ah,' said Constable: 'since what I have to say has nothing to do with your function there, it would be very wrong that the Corporation should be at charges. Kindly ring off at once, and then I will telephone you back.'

Tom rang off at once and within a minute Constable rang him back.

'Now,' said Constable, 'the nature of power. The other day, when you came to luncheon here, you expressed certain opinions as to the random nature of historical events. Presumably these opinions are of some relevance to your thinking on the subject of power?'

'Certainly they are. Power too is a random affair. To begin with, it is almost impossible to see it as concentrated in any definite person or persons, if only because the world has long since become too complicated for even the most determined and intelligent individual to exert his will, except in very limited areas.'

'Illustrate,' snapped Constable.

'This isn't a *viva voce*, Provost.'

'Illustrate ... if you please.'

'Very well,' said Tom. 'Power, in the simplest definition, is the ability to do or to act. You, as Provost of Lancaster, are supposedly the most powerful man in the College. Yet to what extent are you able to do or to act inside it? You can recommend, you can persuade, you can influence, you can intrigue. But when it comes to doing or acting, you cannot even dismiss one of the college servants without seeking ratification from the appropriate sub-committee.'

'I should obtain their ratification if I sought in the right way.'

'That makes you a diplomat, not a man of outright power. It makes your authority purely personal ... the kind of authority that extends only as far as you yourself are *seen*. Since you can make yourself seen over most of Lancaster, we may assume that you keep pretty effective control in that very limited area ... not because you are powerful but because, for the time being, people like to please you. So you'd better watch out, my dear Provost. If your Fellows were to start turning sour on you, you could end your days with your rule confined to a small bed-sitting room at the back of your own Lodge.'

Constable laughed grimly down the line.

'Would you care to expand the thought?' he said. 'To translate it into terms of the national or international scene?'

'Not on the telephone, no. The matter is too distressing. Telephones are only fit for making jokes.'

'But if I were to invite you up here again——?'

'——For lunch one day? With pleasure.'

'Or perhaps a slightly longer visit this time,' Constable said: 'power is a very large subject.'

On the afternoon of the day before Fielding was due to return to Athens, Nicos said to him:

'Let us go to the museum, please.'

They drove to the museum, which was by the entrance to the temple site.

'I have something to show you,' Nicos said.

He led Fielding to the statue of the Charioteer. The face and figure were of bronze so worn and fragile that it must crumble, one would have thought, at a touch. The green skirts would disintegrate like sugar-icing, Fielding thought; and as for the sweet, calm face, one could surely push a finger through it as through a mask of papier-maché.

'I have seen this before,' he said to Nicos, 'but I'm glad you thought of coming here now.'

I'm glad, he thought, because this is a timely reminder: a reminder that the Charioteer, according to Plato, stands for the principle of reason, which reins in the twin horses of the soul. I was in danger, he thought, of giving the wilder horse its head. I was in danger of yielding to desire, infatuation, call it what you will or whatever Plato called it, in danger of letting the reins go and leaving the chariot to run on until it crashed. Not now. Despite what I have seen stretched on my bed or cavorting among the olive trees by the sea, I know that I am a man of reason, and I am keeping a firm hold on the traces. This statue will remind me of that and give me strength—the noble Charioteer of the soul.

'Do you know the story of this man?' Nicos asked.

'I know ... a kind of myth about him.'

'I wonder whether it is the same as mine. In mine he is called Automedon, and he drove the chariot from which the warrior Achilles was fighting. One day, when they mounted the chariot, Automedon to drive it and Achilles just behind him, the horses spoke to Achilles and told him that the day of his death was drawing near. As for us, the horses said, we could run as swift as the West wind, which of all winds is the swiftest; yet even so we could not save you, for it is your fate to be slain in battle, by a god and by a mortal.'

'I have heard that story,' said Fielding, 'but I cannot remember that Automedon had much to do with it, apart from just being there. The passage in Homer which describes it hardly mentions him at all.'

'Automedon loved Achilles and wept for him.'

'Homer says nothing about it.'

'Automedon wept,' insisted Nicos. 'He wept so that he could hardly see to drive the chariot.'

'Who told you this?'

'I know that it was so. When Automedon heard from the horses that his friend was to be taken from him, he started to cry. His face in this statue is calm, because he was a soldier and must not give way, but all the time he was crying inside himself—just as I am crying now—and he could not stop the tears from rolling down his cheeks.'

Fielding turned from the statue to look at Nicos. Two huge tears were rolling down the boy's face, which otherwise, like that of the statue, was quite calm.

'Oh Nicos,' Fielding said; 'Oh Nicos, I must go to Athens.'

He looked back at the statue.

'It's not Automedon,' he said. 'It's a man, any man, driving a chariot.'

'A man, any man,' said Nicos, 'crying to himself inside because his friend must go away, leaving him alone.'

'I must say,' said Lord Canteloupe, 'Maisie really is quite something. She's made me feel positively young again.'

'So you've taken up my introduction,' said Somerset Lloyd-James.

They were sitting in the pavilion at Lord's, watching the first match of the season.

'My dear fellow,' said Canteloupe, 'I'm hardly ever out of the place.'

'Don't go overdoing it ... and for God's sake be discreet. Your Department may not be much in the public eye, but you're not without name and importance, and if you're caught out it would mean a nasty scandal. Which is the last thing the Party can afford just now.'

'Who's going to catch me out? And what if they do? Can't a man have a mistress?'

135

'A minister can't,' said Somerset, 'not even a junior one. These days all public men are supposed to be like the angels —devoid of private parts. And what do you mean, *mistress*? Maisie is a common bawd.'

'I'm thinking of taking her away from Curzon Street and setting her up somewhere else. Just for me.'

'You thelfish old bugger,' yelped Somerset, shocked out of his usual calm: 'I've been going to Maithie for yearth. What would I do without her?'

'I might let you share expenses in the new place. We could work out a rota.'

'It 'ud cost me ten times what it does now.'

'Well, if you're going to be stingy ...' said Canteloupe. 'My God, this cricket match is boring. If it doesn't improve soon, I'm going downstairs to telephone Maisie.'

'She's booked for the whole afternoon. I rang her up this morning myself.'

'There you are, you see. Much better have her nicely set up just between the two of us. Jesus Christ,' cried Canteloupe, vibrating with enthusiasm, 'she really is a bloody marvel. Nothing much to look at, as you said, but for sheer lust-making she's unique. I can quite believe she'd have settled Tom Llewyllyn's hash if she'd only been on for the job. How's all that going, by the way?'

'It's working out just as I hoped it would.'

A man came marching towards them down the rows of empty white seats.

'Your cousin, Detterling,' Somerset said.

'Good afternoon, you two,' Captain Detterling remarked. 'Nice to have cricket starting again.'

'You won't find this very amusing.'

'Anything,' said Detterling, 'would be preferable to what I've just been through with Gregory Stern. Do you know what he's doing? He's decided to set up something called the New Jewish Library, and he's got off to a swinging start by contracting for a three-volume commentary on the *Gemara*.'

'What's that when it's at home?' said Canteloupe.

'The *Gemara*,' explained Detterling, 'is a commentary on the *Mishnah*, which itself is a commentary on the *Pentateuch*. A commentary on the *Gemara* is therefore a commentary upon a commentary upon a commentary. Apart from which, Gregory has also commissioned three new books about Israel, all of them by Rabbis, and an eight-hundred-page study of the Diaspora in Poland from 1840 to 1845.'

'Not like him,' said Somerset. 'He's got the reputation of being the shrewdest small publisher in the game.'

'It's all started since Isobel's been pregnant.'

'No connection, surely?'

'I don't know,' said Detterling. 'He's been hopelessly over-excited about the whole thing. Because Isobel's pregnant, he's suddenly seen himself as a kind of patriarch. He's gone atavistic, you might say. He'll probably end up in the Sinai desert with a tent and a camel before long, but meanwhile he's expressing it all through his choice of these ridiculous books.'

'How long will it take him to go broke?' enquired Somerset.

Detterling turned up his eyes.

'You'll see the vultures hovering when the time draws near.'

'He'll be up there hovering with them,' Canteloupe said.

On the morning of the day on which Fielding was due to lunch with General Grivas, he sent four telegrams from his hotel at Delphi: one to Grivas himself, one to the Grande Bretagne, one to Tom Llewyllyn in London, and one to the firm in Athens from which he had hired his car. Then he got into the car with Nicos and started driving west, heading for the ferry by which they proposed to cross the Gulf of Corinth and land on the Peloponnese, a few miles away from Patras. From Patras they would drive to Olympia, and from there over the mountains to Arcadia, that old country where the shepherds piped at noon.

When Tom Llewyllyn received Fielding's telegram, which informed him that there must now be an indefinite delay before Fielding could meet Grivas, he was both puzzled and annoyed. Why an indefinite delay? Either Grivas would meet Fielding or he wouldn't; there need be nothing indefinite about it. And why the lack of explanation? If it was safe to send telegrams on the subject at all, it was safe to offer a more circumstantial account. The whole matter was the more irritating as time for preparing the programme on Cyprus would soon be running short; and although a postponement would be in order, Tom did not relish the task of telling Constable that Fielding was behaving in a manner which made certitude as to dates impossible and did much to bear out Constable's uncharitable judgments, as to Fielding's obliquity, which Tom had been at pains to refute.

A telephone call to the Grande Bretagne Hotel in Athens revealed that Fielding had left the hotel some three days before. He had told Reception that he would be away at Delphi for one night only, but he had since wired—that very morning, in fact—to say that his date of return was now indefinite. That word again, Tom thought: something must have happened on Fielding's one-night excursion out of Athens to throw all his plans into total confusion. Had he been kidnapped and made to send the wires to prevent anxiety in other quarters? Or was he funking his confrontation with Grivas? Or was he, perhaps, ill?

It was clear that if he had been kidnapped his captors would have made him insert in his telegram a convincing explanation of his inactivity. The absence of any such implied first that Fielding was quite free and secondly, this being so, that he had not explained himself simply because he did not wish to. Whatever had happened to cause the delay was therefore in some sense attributable to Fielding himself and almost certainly something of which he was ashamed. What could one do at Delphi of which one would be ashamed? Very little, Tom thought; it would be interesting to find out. He therefore sent for a guidebook, telephoned through (with some difficulty) to the principal hotel listed at Delphi, and was rewarded by discovering that the kyrios Gray had indeed stayed there for the last three nights. He had left that morning ... with his friend. His friend? Yes, the kyrios had—er—met a friend in Delphi, somewhat younger than himself, for whose accommodation in the hotel, as well as his own, the kyrios had paid before leaving. But where had he gone when he left? The kyrios had enquired the best way to the ferry at Antirrhion, so it was to be inferred that he had gone there.

By this time Tom did not need to be very acute to form a rough idea of what must have happened. Fielding had found something he fancied and driven it off. But why on earth had he driven it off in the wrong direction? Why couldn't he have taken it to Athens, since it was so important that he should go there? However much he fancied his new find, he could surely have borne a few hours' separation while he had lunch with Grivas as pledged. Clearly, something was badly out of order and something must be done. But what? It was a question of mounting an emergency operation to rescue Fielding (and with him his programme), and that meant finding a lot of money, which the BBC could be made to cough up, and a man of resource to send in pursuit, which was another thing again. Tom himself could not possibly go, having much urgent work on hand to get out the first programme in the series. The only person he could think of, there and then, was Captain Detterling (whom one automatically associated with expeditions of this nature), but Detterling was a Member of Parliament, and although he was much given to journeys he might not be able to take off just like that.

However, he was worth trying. A call to Detterling's chambers in Albany raised only a mealy-mouthed and unhelpful manservant, and a call to Gregory Stern Ltd raised only Gregory Stern, who insisted that Tom should listen for fifteen minutes while he read out a synopsis for a book on the Jewish problem in Mauritius. After this, Tom was just about to try the House of Commons, when there was a knock on his door, through which came the Director of Features and a man who looked like an upright crocodile in a bowler hat.

'Mr Llewyllyn,' the Director of Features said, 'something very grave indeed has just been brought to my notice. I can only hope that you will be able to explain.'

I will have this, Fielding thought: I must have it. I am well over thirty years old and such a chance will never come again. I must go on having this for as long as I possibly can.

He was sitting on the steps of the Temple of Zeus at Olympia, watching Nicos, who was standing among broken columns somewhere away by the river. Behind and above the temple a small tree-covered hill rustled in the faint breeze of the afternoon. Tourists pottered singly about, for the most part keeping in the shade of pine or masonry. Only Nicos, standing among the broken columns by the river, remained out under the fierce white sun.

Yes, thought Fielding: I must go on having this for as long as I can. But how long could that be? How long could he exist in this timeless state, measuring the hours and the days only by the recurring rhythms of desire, ecstasy, satiety and then, once more, desire? How long could he stay out of the world, thinking nothing of dates or money or obligations, living only in his coloured dream of love?

General Grivas, Tom Llewyllyn, Gregory Stern. Sooner or later he would have to return to their world and account to them for his absence. To Grivas he had wired that he was unwell and begged to be excused. To Tom he had wired that there must be delay. But sooner or later he would have to approach Grivas again, he would have to beg Tom's pardon for the hiatus (and all too probably for total failure, as Grivas might not prove so amenable to a second request), he would have to go home and propose some new scheme to Gregory and start earning his bread. He looked at Nicos, as he stood by the river Alpheius. How long could he go on having this? The answer was brutally simple: until the cash ran out.

So be it, then. If Nicos would stay with him, Fielding would keep him until the bottom of the purse was in sight. Then he would give him what he could and say good-bye, go back to Athens and start worrying about the bills. These would be heavy, and some of them, like the draft he had drawn on Tom's patience, might never be fully met. But that could not be helped. For the first time in seventeen years he had been in love, and this time he must not toss it away from him, as he had before, he must cherish it with all his strength and resources. The gods had offered him a second chance, which was perhaps the greatest privilege in their gift, and if he spurned it they would curse him for ever.

He left the temple step and walked through the scorching sun to where Nicos stood.

'You will stay with me?' he said. 'Promise that you'll stay.'

'If you will take care of me,' said Nicos, 'I will stay as long as it is permitted.'

'Permitted?'

'We do not settle these things ourselves. You know that. There are powers much stronger than us who settle them for us. They let us meet; they will decide when we must part.'

'The Fates, you mean? The stars? The gods?'

'There is one above all these. Necessity, that is what we have always called it in Greece. 'Ανάγκη,' Nicos said: 'Necessity.'

'I was just thinking much the same thing.'

Necessity. When the money ran out. Necessity was above everything, even above those gods who had given him his second chance.

'But meanwhile we can make the best of the time we have,' Nicos said, and ran his tongue over his lips. 'Nobody knows when Necessity will come, so there is no good thinking about it until it does. We will sleep the night here in the hotel and go on tomorrow. Sleep another night, at Tripolis maybe, and go on again. It is best like that.'

'You think Necessity may take longer to catch up if we keep moving?'

'No. Necessity is everywhere at once. But it is nice to feel free, even if we can never be so.'

'They both remained standing,' said Tom to Patricia, 'both the Director and the crocodile man, even when I offered them chairs. So then I knew something really bad must be coming.'

'Oh, darling . . .'

'But at first it just seemed ridiculous. Apparently Miss Enid Jackson of the Administration Department had written to the National Insurance people to say that I had instructed her that my card had been inadvertently destroyed, and would they kindly issue a new one forthwith?'

'And would they?'

'No. They'd consulted their files and discovered I'd never had one at all. For a long time they'd been making attempts to get hold of me, the man in the bowler hat said—like that letter to Buttock's, I suppose—but they'd never succeeded. Now, at last, they'd caught up, and I must understand that I was to be prosecuted for fifty-two separate offences under the Act—i.e. one for every week that I'd failed to stamp my card over the last year, which is as far back as they're allowed to go. Since the maximum penalty for each offence is ten pounds, I could be fined over five hundred quid.'

'We can surely find five hundred pounds, darling.'

'They can also sue through the civil courts for contributions outstanding—in this case for at least as far back as three years, and possibly for the whole lot.'

'We can still find the money. If you haven't got it all just now, I can sell some of the shares Daddy handed over last year.'

'That was the line I took,' Tom said. 'I got my cheque-book out and asked the crocodile man how much he wanted. Let him name his sum, I said, and go away and leave me in peace. But he said it had gone beyond that now. The due processes of the law had been invoked, he said, and there was no stopping any of it. Then he went away and left me with the Director, who was practically flying round the ceiling.'

'But why?' asked Patricia.

'Ah. This is where it all stopped just being boring and absurd and got absolutely loathsome. I was going to be publicly tried, the Director said. So what, I said: I'd plead guilty, pay up and get out. But for twelve years or more, the Director said, I'd deliberately evaded my obligations as a citizen. Rubbish, I said: it wasn't deliberate, I'd never even thought about it. But you *lied,* he said; you told Miss Jackson your child had torn up your card when you never ever had one. A fraudulent lie—he was squealing with indignation by now—to try and evade paying out money for an invaluable social service. A squalid piece of deceit—*and* I'd had the effrontery to involve the BBC, to try to exploit the Corporation as the agent of my falsehood. I couldn't be trusted, I wasn't fit to work with decent people—let alone to give orders to them—I was evil, I was filth, I was slime ... and I needn't bother to come back tomorrow.'

'But Tom ... He can't do that.'

'He can't but those above him can—and have. There's a clause in my contract, something about my preserving the capacity to fulfil my obligations to the BBC. These, it seems, I have implicitly repudiated by my behaviour. Or so the Director has persuaded the gentlemen upstairs.'

His head drooped and he looked very defeated.

'Tom. Darling Tom. After all your work.'

'I don't think it would ever have been much good. For all their fine talk at the beginning. I think they were going to muzzle the series somehow—they've been making difficulties all along. But there's another thing.'

He told her the story of Fielding, as he himself had construed it, and of his very worrying behaviour.

'God knows what sort of mess he's getting into. I was going to send someone after him—I could have got the BBC to pay. But now ... well, I suppose I'll have to go myself. I can spare a few days, as things are.'

Patricia drew a sharp breath.

'You won't be allowed out of the country. Not if you've charges to face.'

'They'll accept security, I dare say.'

'We haven't the money for you to go gallivanting all over Greece. Not with those fines, and all they're going to sue you for.'

'I can manage ... though I might have to ask you to cash some of those shares. Just as a loan, of course.'

'That was for if *you* needed it. Not for anyone else.'

'But Fielding's an old friend.'

'Dirty pig.' Her face was hard and pinched. 'Running off with some filthy little boy from the gutter. If you go after him, I won't give you a penny.'

'Patricia——'

'—Not a penny.'

'Very well. I'll have to get hold of Detterling and ask him to go. He can probably afford the money. But when he asks me why, in all the circumstances, I'm not going myself, I shall have to grovel ... *grovel* ... and say my wife won't let me.'

Patricia saw the danger signals working in Tom's face and realised that she had gone too far.

'Tom, darling ... I'm sorry I said that about Fielding. I didn't mean it.'

'Yes, you did. I saw your face when you said it. It was

obscene.'

'I was upset, at the thought of you going away. Listen, Tom.' She came very close to him. 'Now that you've left the BBC, it's all over with the series. So what does it matter if Fielding doesn't see Grivas?'

She fingered him crudely and pressed up against him. He backed slightly away.

'It would be nice to know the truth, series or no. And then there's Fielding himself to think of.'

Patricia fumbled with her skirt.

'Do you really think Grivas would have told him anything? And as for Fielding himself, don't you think he might be ... happy ... with this boy of his?'

'Perhaps,' said Tom, looking down to where her hands were working.

'Then forget them all,' she breathed at him. 'You've no need to go to Greece, no need to grovel to Detterling either. Look at me, Tom, and say you'll forget them.'

Tom stared fascinated at her violently circling fingers. 'That's right,' she said: 'look at me, and forget them.'

Fielding and Nicos motored over the mountains, through Tropaia (with its tiled roofs and blue balconies) and Dimitsana (terraced on its citadel of rock), and down into Arcadia, most of which consisted of bare hills, not at all Arcadian. But in the later afternoon, on the road between Tripolis and Sparta, they found a little valley in which were trees, wild flowers and a rocky stream. Here they stopped to discuss the night's harbour.

'Back to Tripolis or on to Sparta? From Sparta we could go to Gytheion or Monemvasia and take a boat to one of the islands.'

'No,' said Nicos quickly: 'no islands.'

'Whyever not?'

'The people are dirty and poor. Besides, there is a lot to be seen here in the Peloponnese.'

'As you like,' said Fielding rather shortly.

He stretched himself in the grass, and Nicos came and lay beside him.

'You are tired,' Nicos said, 'after driving over the mountains.' He stroked Fielding's brow with the fingers of one hand. 'It is a long way on to Sparta. Let us rest here a little and then go back to Tripolis, which is a pretty little town with market places and gardens. In the morning we can decide where to go next.'

'All right.'

The sun was warm and friendly in the evening, and the stream chattered quietly like well-mannered children playing at a distance, whose voices can still be heard though their words can no longer be distinguished. Fielding took the hand that was stroking his forehead and licked the palm.

'You have very soft hands, Nicos. Christopher had soft hands. Warm and soft. You are like him everywhere … here, and here, and here.'

'You have soft hands too, and I like it when you touch me … here, and here, and here.'

So they trifled in the valley till the sun went down, then drove slowly back into Tripolis, where they found a hotel which overlooked a tangled garden in the middle of a small square.

In Athens, Earle Restarick went to the Stoa in the Agora and knocked on the door by the statue.

'News from London,' he said. 'The BBC has dispensed with Llewyllyn's services, and for the time being at least "Today is History" is going into abeyance. The pressure is off.'

'*E finita la commedia?*' said the man with a nose like a hockey stick.

'Yes. I must get back to Cyprus straight away. I want you to do something for me.'

'Ring the curtain down?'

'And re-engage the principal boy. Talent like that must not be wasted. Here is some money for him, and an air ticket to get him to Nicosia.'

Both of which Restarick now gave to his emissary, together with some brief and pointed instructions.

Fielding and Nicos walked up the path to Agamemnon's palace at Mycenae. The backs of their hands brushed as they walked. God, Fielding thought, looking sideways at Nicos, for seventeen years, for seventeen long years I've had nothing like this.

Ahead of them was the Lion Gate, square and flat, and above it two stone beasts craning their chins up on either

side of a pillar. After they had passed through the gate and
up on to the ramparts, they could see south beyond Argos
and Tiryns to the bright bay of Nauplion; while just to the
east of them rose the gaunt hill on which the beacon had
flared blood-red, 3,000 years ago, as a sign to Clytemnaestra
and her paramour that Agamemnon, Lord of Hosts, had
taken ship from Troy.

And to the west, just over the road which led up from the
village, was a car park, into which a Land-Rover now
drove.

'There is a postern gate,' said Fielding, 'at the end of a
long passage which leads right through the heart of the
palace. Shall we go and find it?'

'Let us stay here,' said Nicos, who was watching the
Land-Rover.

A man emerged from this, walked out of the car park
and over the road, and started up the sloping path towards
the Lion Gate.

'I wonder,' said Fielding, 'what the Queen and her lover
must have felt when the beacon flared at last. For ten years
Agamemnon had been away ... "far on the ringing plains
of windy Troy" ... and then, one evening as they were
settling to dinner, perhaps, the beacon blazed.'

But Nicos was not listening. He was walking away from
the ramparts and back to the Lion Gate. The man from the
Land-Rover, a small man with a nose like a hockey stick,
came through the gate, accosted Nicos as somebody known
to him, and began to talk. Nicos nodded two or three times,
then both of them passed back through the gate and started
down the slope. Nicos did not look back to Fielding and
made no sign.

'Stop,' called Fielding, and ran down from the ramparts
and through the gate in pursuit.

Nicos and the stranger with the nose turned to face him.

'Where are you going?'

'I am going away,' said Nicos. 'This gentleman has come
from those who sent me, and says that he is to fetch me
away.'

It was uttered as a simple statement of fact, without emotion of any kind.

'Who ... sent you?'

'I was sent to keep you away from Athens. Now it no
longer matters, and this gentleman is fetching me away.'

'Please, Nicos. Don't go. You don't have to go, Nicos. Please don't go.'

'Why should I stay?'

Nicos and the man turned and walked on down the path.

'But do I mean nothing to you?'

Nicos and the man walked on.

'Don't you understand what you mean to me?'

Fielding circled round from behind the other two and started dancing absurdly backwards in front of them.

'Nicos,' he babbled, 'I have money. I will give you money to stay.'

'This gentleman has brought me money. There will be more, he says. Much more than you could pay.'

'Nicos, you're too kind, too young to talk like that.'

'I am well over twenty. No, not seventeen, as you thought. I am not properly grown you see. I wasn't fed when I was a child, and so now I go with those who will feed me and pay me best.'

'But don't you realise what they'll do to you? The horrible ways they'll use you?'

'What should I care? For this week I have been pawed about and slobbered on and called by a dead boy's name. Next week there will be something else. That is all.'

'Nicos. I love you.'

The ridiculous ensemble (Fielding still skipping backwards) crossed the road to the car park. Nicos went to Fielding's car, pulled out the little bag with which he had been travelling, walked over to the Land-Rover and got in. The man with the nose climbed into the driving seat.

'Nicos,' said Fielding, clutching the door of the Land-Rover, 'say something nice before you go. Say good-bye to me.'

He looked into Nicos' eyes for some trace of pity or regret, however trivial, pleading with his own eye for some token of farewell. But the boy's face was without expression: without love or hate or friendliness or disgust, even without recognition.

'Nicos,' Fielding said, 'do you remember the Charioteer? Surely you meant what you said then? The way you said it——'

'—I was being paid to keep you with me. That is all.'

The engine started. The Land-Rover backed suddenly,

nearly throwing Fielding to the ground, and then roared out of the car park and away down the road.

In the Sterns' house in Chelsea, Isobel was toasting herself some Bath buns for tea. She had always had a healthy appetite, and these days she was positively voracious. As she stood over the grill, relishing the smell of the toasting buns and longing for them to be finished, she suddenly saw, as at a great distance, a flash of blue sea and felt a huge spasm of pain and misery pass through her entire body. It was as though she were being emptied of all capacity for joy or feeling, and emptied physically, eviscerated, at the same time. A sickly smell rose off the buns, then the acrid smoke of burning farina; but this went unnoticed by Isobel, who stood and moaned with her hands clasped to her belly while the cruel blood ran down her quivering legs.

9: Sweet Argos

Somerset Lloyd-James and Lord Canteloupe had dinner at the Connaught Hotel to celebrate. They had avocado pears stuffed with smoked and spiced cod's roe, a soufflé of turbot and lobster sauce, chicken cooked with *pâté de foie gras,* and a magnum of champagne to wash it all down; then they had stewed prunes, because these were good for their bowels, and shared a bottle of Taylor '27.

'So all's well that ends well,' Canteloupe said. 'No Llewyllyn, no programme; no programme, no trouble.'

'Not for a while, no,' Somerset said: 'for a while the official version of the Cyprus business—rational concessions made in response to legitimate democratic pressures—will remain unchallenged. The Department of Public Relations and Popular Media has emerged unscathed, and you can now relax. Until the next time.'

'The next time?'

'There's always a next time in this game. All celebrations

must be provisional, even those at the Connaught Hotel. What's more, the next time may very well come tomorrow.'

'Not Cyprus again?'

'No. I think you've heard the last of Cyprus for the next year or so. But there'll be plenty of other awkward affairs which will need explaining away. After all, Canteloupe, your job is to make the truth comfortable enough for the mass of the people to live with—to make the truth *acceptable*. It won't be long, with things as they are these days, before another unacceptable truth is dumped on your desk for treatment. And you won't be able to evade the issue as easily as we've managed to this time. It was sheer luck that Tom made a fool of himself like that, and even luckier that the Director was a jealous prig who was keen to make the most of it.'

'I must say, I'm surprised he persuaded the high-ups to be quite so fierce with Llewyllyn.'

'I don't know,' said Somerset. 'You see, Tom had committed the most serious error of all—he'd flouted a minor convention. He was too innocent to realise that that's the one thing people won't forgive. They'll forgive a murderer, but they'll never forgive a man who refuses to wear a black tie for dinner. Tom's silly little lie made a mockery of the system.'

'Something in that,' said Canteloupe. 'Tell me, what'll happen to that chap Fielding Gray?'

'He's in luck. Since it's no fault of his that the programme's being dropped, he can just come home and claim the rest of his fee as promised. And talking of him reminds me: what arrangements are you making about Maisie?'

'Why does Gray remind you of Maisie?'

'Another old client.'

'That's just the trouble,' said Canteloupe crossly, '—all these old clients. Maisie say she's going to stay put in Curzon Street because she doesn't want to let her regulars down. Can you beat it? I've offered her comfortable quarters in Hampstead and a very handsome income, but she says that Hampstead wouldn't suit her because she can't stand the sight of all those pinkos in open-toed sandals.'

'So you've offered her *otium cum dignitate*,' said Somerset, 'but Maisie prefers Curzon Street. A true professional. It does my heart good to hear about it.'

'If you ask me, she just likes being on the game. Some of

them do, you know.'

'Then here's to Maisie,' said Somerset Lloyd-James, MP, raising his Taylor '27, 'to dear, plump Maisie, the girl with the crutch of gold.'

'In bumpers,' said the Marquis Canteloupe.

Both men drained their glasses and threw them over their shoulders, somewhat to the consternation of the Americans at nearby tables.

Fielding too was thinking about Maisie. As he lay on his bed in the hotel in which he had taken refuge in Argos, he thought about the warning which Maisie had given him and cursed himself for a fool. 'Don't let them know what's in here,' Maisie had said, running her finger round his chest. But he hadn't heeded Maisie, plump, fond Maisie, he'd ripped his heart right out for them all to get a good look. To get a good look and then spit on it. And then grind their heels in the spit.

And yet, he thought as he poured more brandy, would I have missed it if I could? For although it had all been false from start to finish, it had seemed true at the time. The illusion which Nicos had created had been very lovely while it lasted; and the fact that the illusion had been so cruelly destroyed could not spoil the happiness which it had brought him first. A man might catch a pox, he thought, but the ecstasy he had known while getting it could never be taken away. He, Fielding, had loved a mask, he had loved a dummy with human skin; nevertheless, he had loved.

And another thing, he thought in his misery; there had been appropriate revenge. Years ago he had betrayed Christopher; now Christopher had risen up from the dead and betrayed him. And again: he had used Christopher to make a tale, he had exploited him, in *Love's Jest Book*, to get money and a little fame; and now Christopher had come back as Nicos to exploit him in return—to exploit his love and turn it into money, to use his anguish to make a career. Fair's fair, he told himself: paid out in your own dud coin.

How long have I been lying here? he wondered. I came here yesterday and now it is evening again. I stink. I must get up and wash, go out and eat. Where does one eat in this scabby little town? This Hotel? Class Gamma, the first I saw as I drove in yesterday evening, a den to hide in with brandy bottles, which aren't empty yet. Class Gamma: no food in this hotel, no hot water. Why bother? Lie here, blubbering and drinking and stinking, and let the night come down. I'm ugly; I stink; I'm getting old and rotten. Lie here, wallowing in stink and self-pity. Lie here and rot and let the night come down.

'So it looks,' said Max de Freville in the Dome Hotel in Kyrenia, 'as if something very handsome may come of it. Provided the island stays peaceful and the tourists come back.'

'So what now?' Angela said.

'We stay here a few days longer, to approve the provisional plans for the Casino's equipment and decoration, and to tidy up the financial arrangements. Then we go to Athens to talk with Lykiadopoulos—he'll have to come in as the front name.'

'Why? You seem to have got on very well so far by yourself.'

'They're waiting for me to set it all up and pay for it,' said Max. 'Then, when it's a going concern, they'll grab it. The whole lot, down to the last spare roulette ball. But not if it's owned by a Greek. So we go to Athens and talk to old Lyki and bring him in as front name.'

'Aren't you taking rather a cynical view?' said Mrs Ongley.

Harriet Ongley was of Franco-Russian stock, of English birth, of American nationality (by marriage), and of substantial means (by widowhood). She was an old friend of Max's, having sometimes played, with her late husband, at his chemin-de-fer table in London, and she had run into him quite by chance in Nicosia three days before. She was now spending a few days with Max and Angela in Kyrenia before continuing her tour of the Near East. She had a sweet, round, placid face (young for her forty-two years), shapely and carefully shaven legs, a robust appetite for food, and an invincible belief in human goodness which she somehow contrived to reconcile with a keen intelligence.

'Why should they grab your Casino?' Harriet Ongley went on. 'You're always saying how fond they still are of the British.'

'But even fonder of money. So in a few days we go to Athens to see Lyki. And I think, Harriet, that you had better come too.'

'But I'm scheduled to fly to Beirut, and I have no business with this Lyki.'

'I have good works for you to do, Harriet. I have something right up your street. This morning I heard from an old correspondent of mine—Leonard Percival,' he said aside to Angela, '—who tells me that somewhere near Athens Humpty Dumpty has fallen off his wall and shattered his delicate shell. All the king's horses and all the king's men are of little avail in such cases, but a good, patient woman, Harriet, with loving fingers, might just be able to fit the pieces together. At least she could sweep them up.'

'No more broken egg-shells for me, Max. I've had my share of them.' (Mr Ongley had died of martinis.) 'Why should I bother with this one?'

'A work of corporal charity. You are a Roman Catholic, I think? I should be very grateful,' said Max, 'and very interested to hear how you get on. The case, you see, has a certain fascination.'

And then, carefully playing on Harriet's known reverence for the creative arts and those who practised them, Max began to explain.

The morning after Captain Detterling heard about Isobel Stern's miscarriage he went to Gregory's office.

'I'm very sorry about Isobel,' he said.

Gregory looked up coolly from his desk and fingered his waistcoat buttons.

'It was rather gratuitous,' he replied. 'I'm glad you're here. There are some things to discuss.'

A secretary came in and put a bundle of files on his desk. Gregory started to flip briskly through them.

'During the last few weeks,' he said, 'I've signed some very foolish contracts.'

'The New Jewish Library?'

'Yes. Fortunately it's early days yet, and we can get out of most of them in return for small down payments. This one, for example.' He brandished a file. 'The book on the crucifixion. You were quite right, of course. The thesis is unsound and in any case it has already been stated. And this—the commentary on the Talmud. The printing alone would have cost us a fortune.'

'Why the sudden change of plan?'

'I've come to my senses, that's why. I've been in a state of infatuation which has now been dispelled. Next time Isobel conceives I hope I shall know better. After all, parenthood is a very commonplace affair.'

'Well, don't go too far the other way,' Detterling said. 'Some of those books you commissioned are very promising. That Rabbi who's going to assess the strength of orthodox belief in Israel—that's a book we should certainly do.'

'Granted. And one or two more. But for the most part—fwwhutt.' He thumped his fist on the stacked files. 'Now then. Tom, I hear, has left the BBC, and that also means an end of Fielding's absurdities in Greece. I want a novel out of Fielding in time for publication next spring, and a hefty piece of polemics from Tom for the following autumn.'

'Not much time, Gregory.'

'I know. I want them both to be firmly reminded that work is work—and is not to be confused with silly games in Television Studios and Continental Expresses. So I'm going to insist on an absolute deadline in both cases—but I'm also going to offer them a twenty-five per cent increase on their usual advances. Tom I am going to ring up this minute. Where can I get hold of Fielding?'

Detterling shrugged.

'I suppose he'll come back from Greece in his own good time.'

'I want him back in my good time. That's the kind of thing you're good at fixing. Please see that he gets a message—wherever he is—telling him to be in this office one week from today with a two page synopsis, in type or fair round hand, of an eighty-thousand-word novel.'

Fielding's life in Argos had now settled into a routine. He would get up at about eleven o'clock, hands shaking and head buzzing, breakfast off Turkish coffee and some bread and jam if he could face it, and then drive unsteadily to the palace at Mycenae. There he would sit on the ramparts and look towards the sea, thinking all the time of the days he had spent with Nicos. Later on, when the hour came at which Nicos had been taken, he would go over the scene minutely and in every last detail, acting it out word by word and step by step from the ramparts to the car park. As he did this he would search desperately, in Nicos' remembered face, for some sign that the parting was against the boy's will, for some tiny sign that could mean sorrow or fondness; and then, having failed to find such a sign, he would look south again from the ramparts and sit there till evening.

When the dusk came, he would drive back to Argos, eat some kind of meal in a restaurant, buy a bottle of cheap Greek brandy, and go back to his room in the hotel, where he would lie on his bed and drink the brandy until he fell asleep, which he often did with his clothes on. Next morning he would wake quite early but would toss and groan on the bed until the heat in his little room grew unendurable. Then he would plunge his head in cold water, comb his greasy hair, and stumble downstairs to start his day once more.

'My dear Llewyllyn' (Constable had written to Tom) 'I'm sorry to hear that your series, and with it the Cyprus programme, must be abandoned. It would have been interesting to see what came of Fielding Gray's interview with Grivas.'

Well at least, Tom thought, I am spared having to tell him what went wrong with that.

'But the real point of this letter,' Consable went on, 'is to tell you, unofficially, that it has been decided to offer you a Namier Fellowship at this College. Invitation will be made to you in official form in a few days. I need not say how much I hope you will accept. I might also add that I think a period spent in academic surroundings will provide just the kind of discipline needed to complement the facile distinction of your talents and to enable you to treat worthily of power and correlated subjects, which clearly fascinate you as much as they do me.'

'What's a Namier Fellowship?' asked Patricia, when Tom had finished reading out the letter.

'A three-year appointment during which I should have to undertake some serious line in historical research. I should get a Fellow's stipend and all the rest of it, but I should not be expected to teach or administer. Only to get on with my own work.'

'But what will Gregory say? He wants you to have something ready for him to publish next year.'

'Gregory will have to wait. What I can now propose to him instead is a scholarly dissertation to which I shall have devoted three years' loving and detailed work in the peace and quiet of the fens. Up till now, I've been little more than a political journalist. A typical London opportunist. Now I've got a chance to do something of lasting importance ... with the full recognition and backing of the most famous college in the world.'

'You're going to accept this Fellowship, Tom?'

'Of course.'

'But will Gregory want to publish a ... scholarly dissertation?'

'I want to write one.'

'But Tom ... the money? With all those fines you've got to pay.'

'We shall be much poorer, certainly. But it'll be cheaper, living in Cambridge. And at last I shall have proper work.'

'But it'll mean ... burying yourself ... down there. You'll be forgotten in no time.'

'You don't quite understand, Patricia. Robert Constable is giving me an opportunity—I'm pretty sure he's behind it all—to write about the anarchy which permeates historical processes and the deductions which follow as to the nature of power. Constable does not agree with, in fact he strongly disapproves of, the line which I am going to take. Nevertheless he's giving me a chance to state my case because he thinks that it should be stated. It's a magnanimous offer and a magnificent challenge. I wouldn't refuse it for anything.'

'Tom,' said Patricia stubbornly, 'I think I'm pregnant.'

'Are you indeed? Well, you can be pregnant just as well down in Cambridge as you can up here.'

'Tom...'

She came towards him, smiling her invitation.

'Oh yes,' said Tom, not unkindly, 'we can do as much of that as you want. But we're still going to Cambridge, and there's an end of it.'

Harriet Ongley paused in Athens for just long enough to enquire at the Grande Bretagne Hotel whether there had been any further sign of Fielding Gray. She was told that there had not, but that someone had telephoned for him from London and left a message. This message, which was the one Detterling had been trying to pass on as requested by Gregory Stern, Mrs Ongley read and put into her handbag. She then set out, as instructed by Max, for the Isthmus and the Argolid.

She drove a hired car and sang to herself as she drove, arias from Verdi and passages of counterpoint from Bach. She was very happy because she was going to meet a new and 'creative' person, someone, above all, who wanted her help; for while it was true, as she had told Max, that her husband's deathbed had temporarily drained her of charitable impulse, she was a woman who needed to be needed and she had secretly dreaded the prospect of touring the Near East with no one to mind but herself.

Seeing no necessity to go hungry, she stopped for a substantial lunch at the Xenia in Old Corinth. Then she drove on down the road towards Argos, trying to remember a line which she had read in a paperback translation of Virgil. Yes ... that was it: 'and dying he remembers his sweet Argos'. What a lovely line, she thought, blinking her eyes as she drove.

After a time, she turned left to Mycenae, drove through the village and on up the hill to the palace; and as she got out of her car in the car park, she saw the most extraordinary sight.

A young man was capering backwards down the path from the Lion Gate. He was waving his arms and seemed to be pleading with somebody, though there was nobody with whom to plead. He came skipping on down (still backwards), past the little booth where tickets were sold, over the road and into the car park. Then, at last, he turned, and looked in despair at the only car in the park other than her own. It was as if he were watching someone go to the car, do something and leave it again; and then as though that someone were coming towards herself, for the young man's gaze followed an invisible person across the car park and gradually rose until it met her own. She saw that he had only one proper eye, from which tears were streaming down over a filthy and distorted face.

But now the young man was moving. He staggered across the car park until he came to her own car, through the front window of which he started to look so intently that for a moment Harriet too thought that there must be somebody within.

'Nicos,' the young man said, 'do you remember the Charioteer? Surely you meant what you said then?'

Whatever answer the young man received, it was evidently final and unbearable; for he leapt back from Harriet's car as if he had been shot, and then sank on to the ground, where his whole body heaved and throbbed in a grotesque orgasm of grief. Harriet took a deep breath, then went to stand over him.

'I have a message from your publisher,' she said as firmly as she could, 'which I found in the Grande Bretagne Hotel. You are to present yourself in London with a synopsis for a new novel in four days from now.'

'Christopher, oh Christopher,' whimpered the young man on the ground.

'You're hysterical,' said Harriet. 'You need a bath and some fresh clothes and a meal. We will go in my car to Nauplion, where we will stay in a dear little hotel on that island in the harbour. There you will write a synopsis for your novel, and we will then fly back to London and show it to Mr Stern.'

'Who are you?'

'My name is Harriet Ongley, and I have come to take care of you.' She stooped down and put her face near his. 'Please let me take care of you. Don't send me away.'

She started to stroke the greasy, matted hair and took out a handkerchief to dry the wet, pink cheeks.

'There, there. Time to stop crying. Time to come home and start all over again.'

She moved her face even closer, ignoring the foul breath which came from him, and kissed him on his twisted lips.